**Camilla shrank back against the wall
as the young man knocked the jar
of grog from her grasp and pulled
her roughly into his drunken embrace.**

"Pray unhand me, sir," she gasped, bending her head back from him, repelled by the stench of wine on his breath. Instead he drew her so closely that she screamed out, "Father—Father, please come help me."

Suddenly, as she was near to swooning with fear and disgust, her captor was torn from her and she found she could breathe again. A deep resonant voice said, "Randal, let the wench go! Go to your filthy pleasures. I believe her to be Thomas Fernaby's daughter, and you will leave her alone. You've already ruined the jar she was carrying."

"Alas, I fear Sir Caspar Randal is well into his cups," her rescuer said as he turned to Camilla. "He is never a man to my taste, so call to your father if you should encounter him again. I'm afraid I come seldom to inns and should not be available in such a circumstance."

Camilla looked up at him in dismay. Here she stood in a tavern's dim passageway, her apron splashed and stained with grog, face-to-face with the man she had admired from afar: her Lord of Curzon Street!

Novels by Caroline Courtney

Published By
WARNER BOOKS

CAROLINE COURTNEY

Love In Waiting

WARNER BOOKS

A Warner Communications Company

WARNER BOOKS EDITION

Copyright © 1982 by Arlington Books (Publishers), Ltd.

Cover art by Walter Popp

Cover design by Gene Light

Warner Books, Inc.,
75 Rockefeller Plaza,
New York, N.Y. 10019

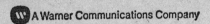 A Warner Communications Company

Printed in the United States of America

First Printing: April, 1982

10 9 8 7 6 5 4 3 2 1

*Love
In
Waiting*

Chapter One

Mrs. Fernaby held the thin, almost transparent hands closely in her own strong ones, murmuring soft words of encouragement. At last, with a moan, the young woman gave birth to her baby. Her tired eyes closed while Mrs. Fernaby tenderly took the new-born infant and did everything that was necessary. Then, advancing to the truckle-bed she addressed the mother.

"Look, lovey, ye've got a beautiful little daughter—I swear she is perfect!" She had wrapped the babe in the swaddling clothes and soft shawl that had been hopefully prepared for a child of her own but, after almost six years of marriage, Mrs. Fernaby had accepted, to her infinite sorrow, that she was destined to be childless.

She and her husband, Thomas, owned The Crown Tavern in Cheapside, the heart of London's East End, but the marriage was not a happy one. Thomas Fernaby took more and more strong ale as the years passed and, when his wife Hannah showed no sign of giving him strong, sturdy sons he berated her and treated her more and more harshly—especially when he was in his cups. Hannah had a heart of gold and made a brave attempt to treat him indulgently, as she might have done a tiresome child, yet was gradually defeated.

So, when she opened her back door one chilly morning to carry washing into the yard, and found a beautiful young girl close to her own in years, lying in a dead swoon on her doorstep, her kindly heart swelled with pity. She gathered the frail body in her arms and carried it up to the small attic bedroom next door to the one she shared with her husband.

After a strong, hot cordial the girl revived a little and opened her bemused hazel eyes, trying to express her gratitude in halting English. Mrs. Fernaby sat down beside her, chafing the cold hands, and vowed that she was now safe and would be well cared for. But the girl started up, her eyes panic-stricken:

"You are *good*—mais I 'ave no money—pas a groat. I—go—on . . ."

"A Frenchie, eh?" asked Hannah, smiling. "Well, I declare we've plenty of food here and more, and I'll not let ye go 'til the babe is come."

Since her husband came to bed fuddled each night, Mrs. Fernaby was able to hide the fact of a non-paying visitor from him. Mrs. Fernaby felt strangely drawn to the hapless girl, lying so quietly next door. And, during the daytime, they managed to talk more easily despite the barrier of language. To her amazement she learned that the girl was a French aristocrat—the Countess de Courville, no less, and that she and her young husband, François, had recently escaped from France after losing all the great de Courville estate close to Paris and their wealth, which had been confiscated by the new republic.

"We—we think we find our—people . . . amis, *friends* —is right now my François est mort—dead? Is consumption, I hear." She turned her head into the pillow and wept. Mrs. Fernaby stroked the long, silken hair, saying nothing for a while.

"Do you know the names of these friends," she finally asked. "Any soul I could send a message to?"

The Countess shook her head and said, in muffled tones, "No. We come—to look . . ."

Hannah Fernaby's heart opened fully then and took

8

both the girl and her unborn child in to fill the great vacuum in her own life.

"Ye'll be safe from now on, I swear it by my faith. Ye have a friend already!"

That evening the young Countess went in labor. She was scarce twenty years old, but the courage she showed proved how much suffering she had already endured. It was not a difficult birth, as Mrs. Fernaby had feared, lasting scarce eight hours, but the young mother had no strength left to survive it—nor the will. She turned away when Mrs. Fernaby offered her the shawled bundle and said:

"Take her, Mrs. Fernaby"—her breath came with difficulty—"Call her—Camilla and . . . is a pacquette . . . in my valise . . . give her later"—then the Countess seemed to rise up a little, her beautiful face shining and, with a cry of "François!" she fell back, dead.

There was no hiding the truth from Thomas Fernaby. Collectors for the paupers grave had to be summoned to take the sheet-wrapped body of the young woman—and there were the demanding cries of a healthy baby that could not be ignored.

When he found that his wife had adopted a girl child—much resented by men of his ilk for they were useless apart from domestic work—his cruelty toward his wife increased.

But Mrs. Fernaby was adamant, finding a courage she had never known before: Camilla was now *her* child, the one so eagerly hoped for and, at last, her life had a purpose, a focus into which she would channel all her love and care.

Camilla Fernaby's eighteenth birthday was fast approaching, and she walked gaily home to the Crown Tavern from the elegant show in Mayfair to which she was apprenticed. It was a distance of three miles but her slender, small body was strong and she had long grown accustomed to the walk night and morning. Her steps grew more fastidious as the ground beneath her changed from immaculately swept pavements to rough cobbles where the gutters frequently overflowed. Unconsciously she held her head high, as the lewd calls of youths began to greet her. They were intended to convey love and longing, only the words disgusted her for they came from the same boys who, when they had all been children, teased and taunted her mercilessly for the clean, pretty dresses over looped petticoats which her mother made for her. Had her fierce, independent spirit needed strength, the battles of childhood turned it into steel.

The girls who used to join in the cruel teasing now watched Camilla passing in silence, their looks half admiring and more than half envious.

For Camilla had grown up from being a pretty child into an extremely beautiful young woman with shining auburn gold hair, wide gray eyes beneath level brows and magnolia skin which highlighted the delicate bone structure of her small face. Her mouth, too, was charming—much given to laughter, and had also grown most tempting. It was this beauty which had first caused Mrs. Fernaby to apprentice her to the Mayfair Shop—a beauty that had, three months earlier, given her husband ideas for making money.

On that fateful evening, Mrs. Fernaby had slipped out after dinner to visit an ailing friend, and Camilla had been left alone with her father in the kitchen to finish the washing up.

It made her both anxious and guilty to feel the fine prickle of fear that ran up her spine whenever she was near her father—surely it was extremely wicked. She was aware, of course, how badly he treated her mother, for the wall between the attics was thin enough to provide easy listening; but she had had no cause herself to feel this fear that seemed beyond her control.

Now Mr. Fernaby leaned on the back of his wife's chair and stared at the girl until she turned to face him. He was

10

not drunk although he had had a few stoops of ale, for it was between noon and three o'clock that his old cronies came to the tavern. In the evening, these days, they felt ousted by the elegant, wealthy young blades who sought constant new amusements for the evening and had discovered The Crown. They demanded wine rather than ale; but it put good money into Thomas Fernaby's pockets so he was proud. He began to grow ambitious for the future since lately the Prince Regent's outrageous extravagances had reached new heights and the sons of wealthy families in society seemed anxious to part with their money for fresh pleasures.

"Did you require something, Father?" asked Camilla, who had never called him papa.

"Ye're a right pretty wench, girl, I'll say that for ye— I'm thinkin' 'tis time ye paid fer yer keep by helpin' me in the tavern o' nights. Aye"—he eyed her up and down in a way that made her cringe inwardly—"Ye'll please the smart custom we get these days."

Camilla paled as she gathered courage. "I will do what I can to pay for myself, Father, but 'twill not be in the tavern! I served ale when I was fifteen if you recall, but the men were too, too free with me, and mama forbade it! I'll not start again now."

Fernaby gave a hoarse chuckle: "Still la-di-dah, eh? Dammit, yer precious *Mama* has bred such superior airs in ye, I declare. Well, ye live in Cheapside so the way she carries on, makin' yer a fine lady and all, be balderdash. 'Tis *me*, at The Crown, has fed ye and kept ye in fancy clothes so now I want *my* share in return—mebbe ye'll catch the eye of some rich ninny who'll wed yer and bring us a fortune. Think o' that, now!" He shrugged his burly shoulders into the broadcloth coat of dark green frogged with braids that hung on the kitchen door and raised his hand to the latch:

"I'm off to the cockfight in the Strand—'tis great sport! Ye should come—mix wi' yer own kind for once. Meantime"—he looked hard at her again and grinned—"ye'll

11

put on yer prettiest gown and be in the tavern tonight, seven o'clock sharp."

Thomas went out, slamming the door behind him.

Camilla sank into a chair, her knees turned to water. She could not, *would* not, run the gamut of serving in the tavern again. The memory of rough, lewd hands grabbing at her skirts as she passed, clutching her young arm as she put down a tankard, made her shiver with revulsion. Yet Thomas Fernaby had the power to enforce his decree since he was her father. She had not fully pulled herself together when Mrs. Fernaby returned.

"What has happened, my love?" she cried, before even removing her bonnet and shawl.

"I am to work again in the tavern tonight," announced Camilla flatly. "Father says I have to pay for my keep."

Mrs. Fernaby had just been present at the sad death of her friend, but love for her dearest Camilla swept all that from her mind.

"You'll do no such thing, daughter—pandering to those young dandies to bring yet more money to my husband! No—bide where you are, I'll make us a dish of tea," she added as Camilla made to rise from the chair and move the kettle from hob to open fire.

Hannah Fernaby swore silently under her breath as she brewed the tea. For the thousandth time over the past years she wished she had somewhere to go—some refuge where she and her beloved foster-daughter could live in peace, free forever from her harsh husband. But there was nowhere. Her friends were many but poor and, deeply as she wished it, she did not know where to seek out Camilla's aristocratic kith and kin.

Camilla's first reaction to her mother's words was gratitude, but this was swiftly followed by compunction as she realized how bitterly Thomas Fernaby would make his wife pay for such disobedience. There had to be some other solution.

"I could tell Father how hard I do work here, Mama," she said eagerly. "Oh, compared to what you do it's nothing, but at least I make beds, clean our rooms—and those four rooms on the first floor where travellers take lodgings overnight. I scrub down the stairs, too, besides sweeping off the dirty sand and laying fresh on the tavern floor while Father is still asleep. Maybe he does not understand these things—or that I do my best to help you in the kitchen."

Mrs. Fernaby brought the teapot to the table where Camilla had placed cups and a jug of milk from the churn while she was talking.

" 'Tis no use, lovey, he'd say that was your duty, not work. He is greedy only for money and more money." She sipped the hot tea, trying to slough off the dreadful weariness that possessed her so often lately although she was not yet middle-age.

Camilla watched her, her gray eyes brimming with sympathy for she loved her mother with all her heart and ached to cheer her and, above all, protect her. Forcing back her own fears for the evening, she sprang up, simulating a gaiety she did not feel.

"Dearest Mama, father is right—I *should* earn money now, but it will all be for you and, one day, I shall buy a fine house where you shall be waited on all day and—and wear beautiful silken gowns while great ladies of the *ton* come to take tea with you!" Her vivid imagination filled with this picture and her whole being came alive with enthusiasm. "Now, how shall I begin? I will not scrub floors but aim higher—far higher." She thought for a moment while Mrs. Fernaby caught her mood a little and admired, yet again, the girl's loveliness which seemed to proclaim her aristocratic lineage with every movement. Laughing, Camilla went on:

"Why should I not be a ladies maid? Mama, pray carry your cup to the Windsor chair and see whether I have the right manner."

Smiling, Mrs. Fernaby did as she was bid.

Camilla took two mincing steps and said:

"Did you ring, m'lady? May I bring you a small tisane,

13

perchance? Your evening toilette is laid out ready and I have placed a selection of dancing slippers for your choice. 'Twill be a grand evening, methinks, with much dancing and we must think of your comfort..." Camilla broke off, her eyes dancing. "Is that the correct style, Mama? I declare, I should enjoy serving a great lady, besides I should be learning all the while."

Suddenly her mother sat bolt upright, smiling.

"I vow you would do splendidly, my love—but you have put a thought in my head that should have been there sooner. Would you truly like to serve the *ton?*"

"Indeed I should."

"Very well. Go put on your new print gown—the colors set off your hair to perfection. Then bring your finest pelisse and straw bonnet for we are going out. Your father has gone to the cockfight, correct?"

Camilla nodded, excitement mounting in her:

"Mama—can you truly work a transformation in my life so swiftly?"

Hannah rose: "Aye, if you don't stand chattering, for we have scant time before your father returns and 'tis a long walk to the West End."

Needing no second bidding, Camilla flew up the outside stair to the attics, her pulses racing. The West End! Why, it was a mythical place, the part of London inhabited by only the very highest members of society, ladies who did not rise before noon and then sallied forth in elegant carriages, clad in silken gowns, to pay calls. While young men, handsome and debonnair as the Beaux she had glimpsed through the curtains leading to the tavern at nights, wore brocaded coats with white silk hose and buckled shoes, and shining, pommaded hair tied back into queues with ribbon!

Within three minutes Camilla reappeared in the kitchen, her print dress as fresh as spring, her lovely hair coiled becomingly under the bonnet. Mrs. Fernaby was waiting in her black bonnet and shawl, hiding a touch of nervousness which assailed her. She was flagrantly disobeying her husband's wishes and the punishment would be harsh but, when Camilla appeared looking so enchanting, she dismissed such selfish misgivings: if her plan were to succeed it could introduce the girl to the world where she rightfully belonged, and not in a servant's position either.

She ushered her daughter out the back door quickly and closed the door.

"Where are we going, Mama? Pray tell me or I swear I shall die from curiosity."

As they strode along, for Mrs. Fernaby set a good pace, she said:

"As a girl I had a good friend, Thomasina Prosser she was then. Of course we dreamed dreams as all girls do—catching the fancy of a handsome passing gentleman, who would raise us to his own high station in life"—she smiled ruefully—"they were foolish dreams since no such men ever came near to Holborn, Cheapside and the like for they were afraid of footpads and robbers." She strode on for a time, traversing the lanes and byways which made the distance shorter and ignoring the increased stench of poverty. Then she went on: "Time passed and we grew to seventeen. I fell in love with Thomas Fernaby—aye, he was a fine young man in those days or so I thought, for he was tall and strong and not then addicted to strong ale. So we were wed. But Thomasina, now, she waited—we were no longer so close for I had many duties to perform, Thomas having just inherited The Crown from his father. Then, one day, she called to see me for a dish of tea and, I swear Camilla, you could have struck me down with a feather! She had accepted the offer of marriage from a gangling pharmacist's apprentice, one Samuel Castle who worked in a backroom in the Strand. I was fair flummoxed, you might say, for 'twas not what Thomasina had planned on at all: 'Come down in your ambitions, then?' I asked. But she just smiled: 'Not at all, Hannah—you'll see.'"

"And what happened after?" asked Camilla, slightly breathless from keeping up with her mother's pace.

"*You'll* see before long," was the smiling answer. "That is, if Thomasina has not forgotten me." For the first time doubt crept into her voice, then she shrugged it off: "But no, I declare we were too close for that—at least she will listen to what I say, I swear to it."

They hurried on in silence. Long before they had covered the three mile distance Camilla's gray eyes were lit with wonder: vistas of well-kept streets and magnificent houses opened on either side of them; smart carriages trotted by and, when a front door happened to be opened a powdered footman stood respectfully at the entrance.

"Oh, Mama—does your friend truly live *here?*" she breathed.

"In finer parts yet," declared Mrs. Fernaby. "Mind you, I have only visited Thomasina once since her marriage, many years ago it was, but she is a kindly soul. Nature doesn't change."

By now Camilla was feeling nervous; her longing to make her life here, in such delightful surroundings, mounted by the minute. But what chance had she, a child from Cheapside, of achieving such glory?

They were walking through the most splendid place yet —Berkeley Square, where carriages passed and repassed, their brass lamps and woodwork polished to a fine sheen matched only by the pairs of high-stepping horses—chestnut, black, gray and brown—whose coats shone with good grooming. On the wide pavements young gentlemen walked in brocaded coats and beaver hats, always sporting a gold-headed cane although their steps were blithe enough.

"Mama—does your friend live *here?*" she whispered in awe.

"Just around the corner, Camilla. Now pray, do not be nervous for I wish Thomasina to see you at your best or, I declare, she will not hire you."

They came to Curzon Row, a narrow, paved place edged with small, elegant shops—dressmakers, milliners, jewellers and, at last a charming bow-fronted window bearing the sign: "Maison Castle. Parfumier."

Drawing a deep breath Mrs. Fernaby pushed the door open, setting a silver bell a-tinkle; instantly, before Camilla could look round at the wonders on display, a door opened from the rear and a small, comfortable figure in a white muslin cap and blue frilled gown emerged, limping a little but supported by an ebony cane.

"Thomasina?" asked Mrs. Fernaby, sure that even now she recognized her friend. For a terrifying moment Mistress Castle stared blankly, then with a flush of pleasure, she cried: "Hannah! By my faith, 'tis you! Come—come quickly into my sitting room, I pray."

As they spoke Camilla had grown aware of delicious fragrances that pervaded the pretty blue and silver decor of the shop and she longed to be allowed to work in it.

Mistress Castle's small sanctum was delightful, too, with wing chairs on either side of the bright hearth where a silver kettle sang softly on the hob; snowy lace curtains covered the window overlooking a small courtyard, and on the table a silver tray was laid with delicate porcelain cups and small plates as well as a silver teapot and cream jug.

Mistress Castle waved Mrs. Fernaby to one of the chairs so Camilla stood quietly near the window.

"Well, Thomasina, I see you have prospered," said her friend, smiling. "I would have called on you before but The Crown has become fashionable these days. Even now I can scarce stay more than a few minutes or my husband will be demanding why I am not attending to my duties!"

Mistress Castle's smile put Camilla in mind of a contented tabby cat as she shook her head. "Oh, I am fortunate, indeed. Mister Castle is mighty forbearing . . ." She waited, expectantly, for Mrs. Fernaby to come to the reason for her visit, so there was no delaying it.

"I am come to ask a favor, Thomasina—may I present my daughter, Camilla? Come forward, child." While Mis-

17

tress Castle looked the beautiful girl over carefully with small, shrewd eyes, her Mama hurried on: "I have brought her up well, you see, feeling certain that she would better herself. Now she is almost eighteen and—and should you need an apprentice I vow you will find her well-mannered, tireless, and an excellent worker."

"Surely she is of great help to you at the tavern?"

"To me, yes. But now my husband wishes her to work in the tavern itself o' nights and I declare it is not seemly. Oh, the young gentlemen are well-bred, I agree, but with her beauty I fear they might consider Camilla fair game when they are in their cups."

She paused, unable to hide the anxiety in her eyes, and Mistress Castle nodded her head wisely. "Indeed, a tavern bar is no place for a pretty girl. Come here, child, since I declare I have not heard you speak! Do you wish to work in a fashionable establishment?"

Camilla instinctively dropped a little curtsey and replied in her low, pleasing voice:

"I do indeed, Ma'am. I vow I have seen no place as delightfully tasteful as yours!" She raised her clear gray eyes and looked full at Mistress Castle. "I wish to work for you very much and am not afraid of long hours."

Mistress Castle nodded, her silvery ringlets shining under the white cap. "I am growing plagued with the rheumatics, Camilla, and have been thinking that young legs in the shop might help me vastly. I must warn you, though, that you have much to learn for we can have no clumsy ways. Mister Castle creates rare, expensive perfumes as well as pommades for gentlemen and delicate toiletries to please the ladies. So, you understand, I can offer no more than a shilling a week for the time being."

Mrs. Fernaby would have protested that her friend was, surely, striking an unfair bargain—she had hoped to tell her husband that the girl would bring two shillings home at least. But Camilla forestalled her: why, to be allowed to spend each day in these surroundings, to traverse the handsome streets and squares outside regularly, was a rare

18

privilege. Indeed, she would have worked for no pay at all.

"That is most generous, Mistress Castle. I will strive to please you, I declare—and I am not fumble-fingered."

Mistress Castle beamed at her.

"I warrant you have sense as well as looks, my dear. I shall expect you at eight o'clock tomorrow morning." She turned to Mrs. Fernaby. "May I offer you a cup of tea, Hannah? 'Tis quite a step from Cheapside."

But Mrs. Fernaby had risen, torn between relief and a sense of grievance at her friend's niggardly offer.

"Thank you, no. We have scant time to get back before opening time as it is."

Camilla sensed the coolness in her mother's voice and added warmly:

"You have been goodness itself, Mistress Castle. I shall be here punctually, I swear."

When they had left Thomasina Castle she went in search of her husband who toiled from dawn to dusk in his spotless pharmacy, pounding rare herbs, spices, and flowers together in a large pestle ready to create, as only he knew how, new fragrances to please the gentry.

"I have struck a fine bargain, husband," his wife declared. "For but a shilling a week—scarce the price of one cake of soap—I have engaged the loveliest girl you ever did see to help in the shop. Well-mannered and pleasantly spoken she is."

While she related what had happened, Mrs. Fernaby and Camilla were hurrying through the lanes and byways toward The Crown at even greater speed than they had come.

"Oh, Mama," cried Camilla, her eyes shining with gratitude, "I will work harder than ever to help you in the evenings now—for I can never repay you enough for such a chance! Why, I shall be serving all the great ladies in society—and gentlemen, too. And I swear I have never seen a shop so pretty!"

Her mother had not the heart to voice her inner grievance—and, with a pang, she decided that if Thomas per-

19

sisted in demanding Camilla's presence in the tavern at night, she would ask Thomasina to board and lodge the girl once she had proved her worth.

He was waiting when they entered the kitchen, his face red with anger.

"Cavorting, eh? No tea prepared and the fire dead as mutton! 'Tis an outrage and I'll have no more of it! Get to work, woman, and you, girl, make yerself prettified for the gentlemen."

"I am not working in the tavern, Father," said Camilla clearly. "I have secured fine employment this very day in the West End and in such time as I have I shall help Mama as usual."

His small, bloodshot eyes opened wider in astonishment.

"Dammit! I'm in half a mind to beat ye, girl—when I give orders I'll not be disobeyed." He banged his fist on the table. *"I tell you, you'll work here—for me!* Up West, indeed! 'Tis more of yer mother's hoity-toity nonsense, eh? I'm good enough to be yer father—oh, aye, that's mighty convenient, ain't it? but I declare ye're a disobedient brat and ye'll be in the tavern this night or 'twill go ill for ye!"

Mrs. Fernaby's eyes gleamed like a tigress defending its young. "I'faith, she'll do no such thing. 'Tis a fine position she has now—*and* she'll bring home good money since that's what you're after!"

"How much?" He turned on his wife belligerently.

Before Camilla could open her mouth her mother snapped, "Three shillings!"

It was pretty fair money for a youngster and surprised him.

"Well—I warrant ye'll hand it over to me every Friday, girl. Tho' I swear ye owe me a mint from all ye've had over the years. And wife, since she's going to *help* you"— his tone sneered—"I'm thinkin' we should serve tasty pasties and such in the Tavern o' Nights. Like bean poles, them young gentlemen are, but they eat their heads off. D'ye know the Prince serves *eighteen* courses o' fine vittals every night o' his life? So get on with it—ye'll make pheasant pasties with other rich game in 'em, too, and I'll make the young dandies pay well!" He went out.

"Oh, Mama! How can I give him three shillings a week?" cried Camilla. "And he's given you yet more work to do!"

"I warrant I'll manage," answered Mrs. Fernaby grimly. "I can make the extra with my sewing, and as to the pasties—well, he'll not get such a good dinner himself, there'll be no time. No, lovey, I want the very best in life for you, and in that shop ye'll meet yer own kind."

"My own kind? I declare I don't understand." Camilla was puzzled.

Swiftly her mother turned away, busying herself with hanging up her bonnet and shawl, horrified at her slip of the tongue. Camilla would have to know her true origins soon but not yet—not quite yet—not until her eighteenth birthday in three months time. It was selfish, possibly, but Mrs. Fernaby had always feared that once Camilla knew the truth of her background, she might accuse her of not finding an aristocratic family in which to bring her up— and this would be beyond bearing.

"Now, we must set to cover those pasties," she said briskly, rolling up her sleeves. "I'll see to them if you'll slip along to the market and see what Mr. Potts has left— pheasant, duck, or hare, 'twill all be the same once I've seasoned and spiced it well."

Camilla slept little that night. Would she please Mistress Castle, she wondered. And how, if her father took the wages, would she ever be able to rescue her beloved mama? Her fitful dreams alternated between elegant young gentlemen with carriages in Berkeley Square to the vicious, bloodshot eyes of Thomas Fernaby. From now on she would be living two very different lives.

21

Chapter Two

Camilla set off from The Crown at seven o'clock the following morning. It was a beautiful April day with white clouds in an azure sky and sunlight touching even the meanest buildings with gold. Her mother had given her a small parcel of pasties left over from the night before.

"Thomasina is becoming something of a skinflint, I fear, and she may expect you to bring your own dinner," she said. Then, hugging her foster daughter—a rare gesture indeed—she added, "Do well, little love, for I declare you will please the gentry."

The distance seemed shorter than it had the previous day and Camilla began humming softly under her breath; there would be no scrubbing stairs today for she was about to enter a whole new, magical world in the chic Maison Castle where the grandest people in the land would come.

Whom would she serve first, she wondered? A duchess? But no, they rose late in the morning. Some young dandy, perhaps? Her mouth curved in a delicious smile: she would bob the little curtsey that had pleased Mistress Castle and offer him a selection of the very finest pommades. She hoped he might be dark, since men with black hair and brown eyes always seemed to her much stronger than their equally handsome fair counterparts.

As she entered the West End by herself she was surprised at the greetings she received—as though she were familiar to them already. A young footman, not yet powdered but wearing a striped waistcoat, as he polished a brass doorknocker, paused to stare. Then he called out blithely, "Why so much hurry, Miss? Got no time for a kiss, eh?"

She tossed her head and walked on, her cheeks flaming. But soon she grew accustomed to it. After all, the grand ladies were not yet astir and it proved that she must be pretty. A lad delivering fruit and vegetables tossed her an apple.

"The best o' the lot—but ye deserve a peach!" He grinned and Camilla caught the fruit, smiling her thanks.

I am one of them now, she thought, as she parried merry whistles and flirtatious suggestions, usually given with a wink. I *work* here! It filled her with pride and new confidence—these grand streets would soon be as familiar as Cheapside, and she arrived outside Maison Castle with ten minutes to spare.

Mistress Castle still in her peignoir and lace mob cap, greeted Camilla. "Good, good—you're punctual Camilla. My rheumatics are plaguing me this morning, I declare, so I'll just sit here and teach you your duties while I rest a little. We don't open our doors until nine o'clock—fine customers are rarely abroad by then and only the cream of society give us their patronage." Her smile was smug, self-satisfied at having cheaply acquired a girl to undertake the most tiresome tasks. Yet her eyes were not unkindly and Camilla was only too anxious to please. Everything about the chic little shop appealed to her inner senses: the charm of the blue and silver motif, the delicate scents, the cleanliness (so different from old sand on the floor at The Crown) and, above all, the expectancy of the first fine customers.

Mistress Castle settled herself in a chair behind the counter and issued orders:

"Through in the kitchen—yes, straight through my sitting room—you will find fresh, fine dusters on the small line above the range. Bring them and carefully dust each phial of perfume on the shelves, then all the other goods. Twice a week you will remove everything and thoroughly wash the shelves themselves . . . ."

Camilla moved swiftly, but never clumsily as she followed directions. The phials of perfume were exquisite, she thought—little flasks of Bristol blue glass with silver stoppers and exotic names on the labels: "Hibiscus," "Night Primrose," "Acanthus," "Oil of White Lilac" and many more—some even bore the names of goddesses such as "Eau d'Aphrodite." The prices made her eyes widen for some were as high as two guineas! She grew curious about Mister Castle for he seemed something of an artist, too, since sweet smelling soaps were shaped like flowers while pommades and hair oils for the gentlemen were contained in miniature decanters of clear crystal.

When all was done to Mistress Castle's satisfaction she eased herself up. "That is a good beginning, Camilla, for 'tis scarcely half past eight. Now, while I dress I pray you see to your hair. There is a mirror in the kitchen and it is *comme il faut* for high-class shop girls to wear ringlets. Oh, and that dress will not do—no, not at all. 'Tis out of fashion, I declare. Pray inform Mrs. Fernaby that I require a pale blue print, the skirts shaped over small hoops, and a white muslin fichu at the neck." She turned away.

But Camilla would have none of it. Standing very straight, her gray eyes flashing she said firmly, "I fear that is not possible, Mistress Castle. Mama works far too hard at the tavern to sit sewing gowns to please you. And one shilling a week will scarce pay for print or muslin!"

In that moment she did not care if Mistress Castle dismissed her. Crisis hung in the air before the older woman turned: "So—you have a duty to your dear mama, and fine spirit too. Pray do not show such spirit to the customers; they prefer quiet, deferential manners no matter how much they fret and fume over a purchase." She sighed dramatically. "I fear there is nothing for it but to send you to my dressmaker for the suitable dresses, but I shall send

24

a note instructing her to use the cheapest print and I fancy I have an old lace curtain set aside which will serve for the fichus. Now, see to your hair and stop chattering!" She went out with an air, leaning on her cane.

Camilla smiled to herself. So Mistress Castle would try any ruse to save a penny or two, but standing up to her was not dangerous.

Then her mood changed to panic—ringlets! Her hair was so thick and lustrous Mrs. Fernaby had always brushed it back, tieing it with a wide ribbon. In the kitchen, peering into a small mirror on the wall, she tried again and again to twine strands around her fingers but even when she moistened them with water from the tap they would not stay in shape. With tears of vexation in in her eyes she stamped her foot.

" 'Tis useless! They will *never* obey me!"

A gentle voice behind her startled her and she swung round.

"Nothing is ever *useless,* my dear. What troubles you?"

The question came from a tall, thin man with stooping shoulders and strands of silvery hair brushed over his balding scalp. "You must be Camilla Fernaby—allow me, I am Samuel Castle." His pale eyes were as gentle as his voice. "Can I be of assistance?"

"You are very kind, Mister Castle, but I warrant nobody can . . . Mistress Castle bade me make ringlets but my hair is quite wrong."

He raised a blue-veined hand and touched her hair without seeming familiar and he smiled. "It is extremely beautiful hair, my child—exquisite texture and too silky for ringlets, I swear. Pray sit on this stool for I declare a different style would be becoming. I am a pharmacist, you know," he added, "and hair I understand very well."

Sitting on the stool Camilla felt a great warmth for the old man.

"I know you do. Indeed, you create all the wondrous things in your shop, do you not? All those perfumes and toilet preparations."

"It's pleasure, also, as well as work," he assured her as he busied himself arranging her hair smoothly back into a chignon on her neck. "Now we must borrow pins and a cap from my wife's little store in here . . ."

At last he was done and one of Mistress Castle's muslin caps was tied under her chin. He lifted the mirror from the wall and offered it to her. "I hope the effect meets with your approval?"

Camilla gasped with pleasure. "Why, it is most becoming, I declare! But—but will your wife not be angry?"

Just then Mistress Castle bustled through the door and stared.

"I happened by chance on Camilla, my dear," said her husband, "and the ringlets were atrocious so, knowing hair as I do, I ventured to interfere. Does she not look charming?"

Camilla learnt then with what high regard Mistress Castle held her husband and that his word was law. Surveying the result, all smiles, she nodded several times. "How very wise you are, Samuel—'tis most unusual."

Mister Castle had set the cap far enough back to show a sweep of glorious auburn gold hair with two tendrils curling delicately on either side. The chignon was neatness itself, while still highlighting the beautiful coloring.

And so Camilla started her first day as a shop assistant.

As a silver clock struck nine, Mistress Castle indicated that Camilla should open the street door that stood between two pretty, bow-fronted windows framed by white curtains looped back with blue ribbon and displaying from within a choice selection of the wares. As she drew back the bolts and turned a heavy key, Camilla felt a flutter of nervousness. Fervently she prayed that Mistress Castle might receive the first-comers to show her the right thing to do.

But no one came. Time crawled by until ten o'clock struck and still no custom which increased Camilla's timidity since Mistress Castle sat reading the *Court News Sheet* and the silence grew oppressive.

26

At last the shop bell tinkled and two young gentlemen strolled in, one yawning widely without putting up his hand. "Lud, Christopher, playing cards with Prinny at Carlton House takes it out of a fellow, don't yer know?"

His companion, stocky and fair with a humorous grin said: "I warrant you lost, eh? And drank overmuch claret?"

His friend sighed with some exaggeration, "Fifty guineas—half my monthly allowance. I declare, His Royal Highness cheats abominably before he leaves for Brighton! Fancies our shekels, I warrant. But the claret isn't half bad."

"If you don't overdo it," chuckled the stocky man. "You can still afford Castle's Pommade?"

"M'dear Bonzo, a chap can't appear at a ball without it —I am bidden to Lady Ankerton's affair tonight." He yawned again and moved languidly to the shelf of pommades, adding: "The shockin' efforts she makes to marry off that suet dumpling of a daughter are laughable. The champagne is damn good, though." He picked up one little crystal bottle after another and Camilla, standing quietly in the background with her eyes shyly lowered so that she could watch through her long lashes, feared he might drop one. But he soon made his choice and sauntered to the counter where Mistress Castle summoned the girl to attend the purchase.

Camilla wrapped the parcel in blue paper tied with silver ribbon, feeling some confusion since the merry eyes of the gentleman called "Bonzo" were fixed on her appreciatively.

Giving the small bob curtsey she handed over the parcel and said,

"That will be one guinea, if you please, sir."

"Strap me! A guinea," grumbled the world-weary customer drawing out his purse. " 'Tis fortunate for Mister Castle that he is so *à la mode,* but I swear his stuff will be aped more cheaply in a short space."

Remembering kindly, gentle Mister Castle, Camilla's

27

temper rose in defence of him and she would have given a sharp retort, but Mistress Castle was keeping a wary eye on this, her first sale, so she kept her lips firmly closed.

After the young blades had left she turned swiftly. "Pray, are all the young gentlemen so ill-mannered? And saying wicked things about our prince, too!"

"To such as them pay no attention, my dear," Mistress Castle advised in honeyed tones. "They are of no consequence but, praise heaven, at least they *pay*. As for the Prince—well, my child, I warrant you will hear much gossip from our clientele—they appear to believe that shopkeepers have no ears!"

"But—to say that he *cheats* at cards is infamous!" cried Camilla, bewildered. Mrs. Fernaby had brought her up with great respect for royalty.

Any reply was cut short by another tinkling of the shop bell. By then the hour was eleven and young ladies often sauntered out to purchase a few fal-las before taking morning chocolate together. The three girls who came in were much her own age, yet their morning toilettes struck Camilla with awe: long redingotes of colorful cloth over ankle length skirts, expensive fur tippets against the spring breeze, with high bonnets decked with beautiful feathers and edged with matching fur. They wore soft kidskin gloves and carried reticules of fine gold mesh. Being young they were eager and not at all intimidated so Camilla moved forward, anxious to serve them.

Their voices were high-pitched. "Oh, Miss Castle, we require elegant perfumes for a ball—pray assist us to choose," said one, her blue eyes alight with daring. " 'Twill be our very first ball, I declare, and Maison Castle, so Mama tells me, is *crême de la crême.*"

Camilla forgot her nervousness and entered into the adventure, although she was not yet totally familiar with all the perfumes. Yet they were easily satisfied and thanking her effusively paid two guineas each for their precious purchases.

Grudgingly, Mistress Castle complimented her, but

added, "This afternoon we shall receive great ladies and young lords, so pray do not think that one success will do."

Camilla would not have been invited to take dinner with them, and she was very hungry, but for the quiet intervention of Mister Castle who insisted that the new apprentice had earned a hot meal.

That afternoon, indeed, two of the most elegant ladies Camilla had ever seen came to Maison Castle and even Mistress Castle gave a small curtsey, addressing one of them as Your Grace. With them came a lady's maid carrying a shallow wicker basket to carry their purchases. Their hats were a revelation of feathers, flowers, and veiling to protect their coiffures from any breeze. Diamonds sparkled in the lace fichus, and matching large brooches were pinned to the fine grosgrain-silk of their chic fitted coats over matching skirts. The Duchess—for what else could she be—wore a lorgnette of tortoiseshell on a long gold chain and, through this, she frankly studied Camilla who stood well back, her eyes downcast.

"H'm," came the verdict at last. "I warrant you have a young girl of some beauty to assist you, Mistress Castle. I trust you will not allow her to encourage the foolish young beaux who have more money than sense to patronize your shop more frequently!" It was a haughty reproof and Mistress Castle flushed red.

"Most certainly *not,* Your Grace, by my faith. The girl is daughter to a friend of mine who has fallen on hard times. She is in no way forward, but of good character and a shy disposition."

"Glad to hear it." The Duchess snapped shut her lorgnette and demanded to be shown the latest creations in perfume by Mister Castle.

Camilla's anger rose during this exchange—how *dared* Mistress Castle describe dear mama as "fallen on hard times?" But she was learning—oh, yes, she was learning a great deal about Mistress Castle and, above all, she knew that she wanted to go on working there beyond everything.

Within two weeks Camilla was completely at home in the shop, no longer allowing Mistress Castle to distress her. A shy friendship grew between her and Mister Castle whose spotless pharmacy pleased her finest sensibilities. He even gave her the honor, now and then, of asking her opinion on his latest creation.

Besides, another part of her life in the West End was opening up: dreams. She was often sent on errands or to deliver a package to some great house and, as she grew more familiar with the handsome streets and squares, as well as the sight of smart carriages and beautifully dressed people, a strange feeling pervaded her. *I belong here,* she thought in amazement. *This is my world and, one day, it has to be.*

She said nothing of this to Mrs. Fernaby when she returned home and, after standing for a few moments on the corner of Curzon Street while some returning riders from Rotten Row in Hyde Park trotted to their stables, Camilla stood riveted to the spot. A most distinguished carriage, painted very dark green, stood at the curb with a fine pair of matched grays.

After a pause, a front door between two splendid white pilasters opened, held by a footman. With light strides a young man emerged, turning slightly to throw a final order over his shoulder so that Camilla saw his face and her breath caught in her throat. He was vastly different to the young dandies who came to the shop; tall and lean as a whiplash, thick dark hair held back in a queue with a wide black bow, dark eyes, and a some-what olive skin over the most handsome face she had ever seen. His coat, although less flamboyant, seemed richer by far because of its simplicity—dark green broadcloth frogged with black braid fitting closely to his slender waist while his flawless breeches, without a single crease, ended not in fancy garters but were met by the tops of soft, doeskin boots. He leapt into his carriage, giving an order to the driver who actually turned and smiled, touching his cocked hat. So far Camilla had never seen a driver smile at his patron.

Slowly she released her breath, her eyes shining under her bonnet since she had just glimpsed the man who could, by a look, capture her heart forever.

From that moment on her romantic fantasies had a central character: as was told in the old fairy tales, she had seen her prince.

After that day she seized eagerly on any errand that could take her near Curzon Street, often waiting on the corner as long as she dared. The days when he didn't emerge were gray indeed but at least three times he did, and she wondered afresh as to what set him as a great gentleman apart from all the others? 'Twas not his elegant, sober dress but more his lithe movements, so assured of willing service, they proclaimed his natural aristocracy beyond question. She gave him many titles, none ever seeming grand enough to do him justice—a duke, perchance? Or even a foreign prince with that dark complexion? Then she decided that he was a lord since, though not so grand, the word seemed to fit him.

Sir Michael Monford himself never even noticed the shy girl on the corner. At twenty-eight he was heart-free, although he attended balls and was much in demand at dinner parties for his interesting, witty talk. Added to which the daughters of most noble houses were more than half in love with him. Accustomed to the flowery phrases of their usual beaux, Sir Michael's slight aloofness intrigued them mightily. For he flirted not at all, never feeling sufficiently attracted to any young socialite he had met so far; besides, his life was full of interests and it was early to think of marriage. Sir Michael kept a stable of four fine horses and rode superbly; he also read widely being particularly interested in history and fine poetry. Now and then he visited his country estates in Berkshire where his mother presided over the beautiful manor house and entertained the county for her daughter, Augusta. Sir Michael was fond of his sister but some of her ways exasperated him: at twenty she was plain and overweight, unashamedly enjoying rich pastries and sweetmeats; with thoroughbred horses at her command, she hated riding or any exercise other than dancing a trifle awkwardly. When they wished to shop in London, Lady Monford and Augusta stayed at the house on Curzon Street but their visits were rare, merely ordering the latest gowns to suit the coming season of the year.

Yet Camilla, now wholly in love with the unknown man, feared that anyone so handsome must have a wife even though she never saw him escorting a young beauty when he went out.

More and more the West End life lured her, however, strengthening her ridiculous inner feelings that she *must* belong there. How could she, daughter of tavernkeepers in Cheapside, *possibly* belong to the *haute monde?*

Meantime, it seemed to Mistress Castle that more young gentlemen than before came to the shop and, without fail, eyed Camilla boldly. Anxious not to offend her most illustrious customers such as the Duchess, she said tartly one day, "I declare, I cannot be after you all the time, child—my rheumatics need rest. But I trust you do not encourage the young gentlemen with unseemly looks?"

Camilla's spirit rose and she flushed with anger. How *could* she encourage such ninnies when her heart had found its ideal?

"Most certainly I do *not*, Mistress Castle! Indeed I do not give a fig for them! I serve them politely, as you would wish, and that is an end of it!"

Mistress Castle was forced to believe her, since her husband liked the girl and had expressed his high opinion of her on many an occasion: "Camilla may be your friend's daughter, m'dear, but I warrant she has the behavior of a young lady."

On her way home one evening, Camilla came on a splendid sight in Berkeley Square: a red carpet stretched from the doorway to the curb, protected by a red and white awning in case of inclement weather. Every window in the mansion blazed with light from crystal chandeliers and soft music floated out. Camilla stood spellbound, watching as carriage after carriage set down ladies in ball gowns ablaze with jewels—some still preferring the white peruke with jewelled conceits in front. All were escorted by gentlemen in fine array who handed them out with as much care as might be given to spun glass and offered a courtly arm to the door.

Would her "Lord" appear? And would he, too, have a lady on his arm? But, after twenty minutes he did not come and Camilla, with a start, realized that mama had asked her for extra help in the kitchen that night and time was growing late.

She ran almost all the way home, her thoughts bedazzled by the fine sights she had just seen. And it was just as well that she arrived a little late.

For Thomas Fernaby had announced a new plan to his wife: "My mind is made up, wife, and no matter what paltry excuses ye offer, 'twill not change!" He sat heavily in the wicker kitchen chair. "Trade is prospering to my profit but there are good, golden sovereigns to be made each night and I'll have 'em I swear."

Mrs. Fernaby, already tired with much cooking for the tavern, leant against her table for support and asked, "I trust you make no further demands on my pasties, Thomas, for 'tis not humanly possible."

"Pasties?" He threw back his head with a throaty chuckle. "No, no—'tis dishes of a different sort I mean to offer the young gentlemen. They'll not long be satisfied by finding good wine in Cheapside—they seek further inducement." He pretended to reflect, then: "The travellers who take rooms on the first floor earn little profit—'tis four good rooms going to waste, so we'll take no more of 'em. No, Hannah, we shall turn those rooms into a bordello! A whole golden guinea for each 'gentleman' who wishes to patronise it." He puffed out his red-veined cheeks with satisfaction. "The Crown Bordello—it has a goodly ring to it, and I wish those rooms made prettified within three days since I mean to spread the news this very night!"

Mrs. Fernaby thought she would faint from shock and revulsion. "A—a *bordello*—here, under our very roof? Oh husband, you cannot mean such wickedness? 'Tis unthinkable."

When Thomas Fernaby stood up he was formidable and he did so then, his small eyes glinting with greed.

"Ye do not move with the times, wife. His Royal Highness whores and wenches where he pleases and his young dandies insist on the same. I'll not hear ye're silly preachin' —wickedness, indeed! 'Tis nought but fashion, and why should I not reap the gold? Those rooms will be ready, I vow, or 'twill go hardly for ye."

"I'll have no part of it, Thomas," commanded Hannah, gray to the lips. "Nor, if ye carry on, will I have sich girls in here!"

He moved heavily toward the door to deliver his final blow: "Cleaning the rooms is the brat Camilla's duty— her, with her hoity-toity ways. I'll get the girls—Peg of Holborn is willing, and young Joan up the way is glad to ply her trade in a dry bed rather than in a doorway. But there is a bit more—I insist that our 'daughter' shall be the main attraction!"

"You shall not do sich a thing, Thomas." Hannah was now white with fury—and fear. "If ye touch my Camilla I'll run ye through with the meat knife, I swear by the Holy Jesus!"

"Swear all ye like, wife—she owes me for a lifetime o' good vittals. 'Three shillings a week' she gets—why, 'twould not feed a pullet! No, in the bordello she'll reap good gold for me, and I am determined!" He slammed the door behind him.

Hannah Fernaby sank down into the wicker chair, her body numbed by shock. A bawdy house—all those hateful antics going on just below her own bedroom! But that was as nothing compared to the threat to Camilla.

In three days the bordello must open, Thomas Fernaby had decreed—why, that would be on Camilla's eighteenth birthday! Fear and despair overwhelmed Mrs. Fernaby;

she had been storing small gifts for many weeks, pretty ribbons, two lawn handkerchieves she had embroidered, a little reticule bought from a Barrow for a few pence, and half dozen other trifles. She had planned, too, to bake a cake which she and Camilla would enjoy when the evening's work was completed and Thomas had stumbled up to bed.

And now Camilla would have to leave—have to leave the tavern for her own safety and stay with Mistress Castle.

At last Hannah Fernaby wept, all the trials and tribulations of her life since marriage gathered into this final tragedy—losing the daughter of her heart. Even her inmost revulsion against the bordello seemed as nothing compared to that.

Then a glance at the clock told her that Camilla should soon be home so she washed her face at the sink, forcing back the agony of mind, and bent to her pastry praying that her recent tears would not be obvious when the girl returned.

Camilla, her mind full of the people she had watched arriving for a ball, for once did not pay much attention to her mother's appearance. Instead, as she donned her long apron to help with the pastries, she wanted to share these wonders of society with her dear mother.

"The *gowns*, Mama! Such glorious stuff and colors as I have never dreamed of here—why, one silk was so splendid it changed from a myriad of blues to greens as the lady moved, then back again. As to the diamonds, they would have bought all Cheapside, I declare! Some were as large as pigeons' eggs, and the gentlemen were just as sumptuously dressed in brocaded coats embroidered with gold or silver, and jewelled garters below the knee as well as big diamond buckles on their shoes!" She sighed again at the vivid memory and laughed, "Oh, what a world it must be, I declare! To live with such luxury at one's fingertips to choose from, then sleep until noon knowing that a carriage would await one's pleasure."

35

With a touch of pride she added, "And all those ladies and gentlemen scented by dear Mister Castle!"

"I trow you are fond of him, are you not daughter?" asked Mrs. Fernaby as she worked. "How like you his wife?"

"Mistress Castle is like putty in his hands, I vow, and now that I have been her assistant these three months she seems pleased with me—tho' she keeps an eye open when I serve the gentlemen; but 'tis unnecessary since they are but spoilt children!" Camilla's laugh was indulgent and she held secret her growing love for the Lord of Curzon Street; never, never would she breathe such a thing even to the woman closest to her—it was too unlikely, too far in the realms of miracle, that she should ever meet him . . . .

They pressed on with the arduous task of the pastries and further delicacies ordered by Thomas Fernaby such as oysters rolled in strips of bacon and fried.

Mrs. Fernaby's heart grew heavier and yet Camilla's chatter had done much to reassure her on the girl's behalf. Since the Castles had come to value her, surely they would not deny her a home if need be? Her own grief should be a very private affair once the precious child was far from danger.

To her horror, Thomas Fernaby suddenly appeared in the kitchen to fetch the jar of grog, a thing he normally requested to be brought up to the tavern and his wife shook from head to foot: would he place his plan before Camilla straight away?

But he only paused long enough to stare at the girl afresh. Then, with a leering grin, he took up the heavy jug and said: "Aye, pure gold 'twill be."

There was no choice. Camilla would have to go.

Chapter Three

On the morning of her eighteenth birthday Camilla woke to find her bed surrounded with charming, small gifts from mama and her heart lifted with love and delight, wondering how they had been placed there without her hearing even Mrs. Fernaby's light step in the room.

She could not know that, in order to save her daughter from such humiliating work, Mrs. Fernaby herself—weary though she was—had been preparing the now hateful first floor during the early hours of each morning when her husband was snoring and Camilla in the deep sleep of a child. On impulse she had decided to put out her little birthday gifts for Camilla first thing instead of keeping them until evening. Much might happen before that time came.

Indeed, it was to prove the most eventful day of Camilla's life, but not in the way her mother most feared.

As soon as she arrived at Maison Castle she was greeted with a smile and Mistress Castle gave her a small package saying, "Best wishes for your birthday, Camilla. I declare, you are a good girl and of great assistance." Inside was a cake of soap delicately shaped as a primrose.

"Oh, Mistress Castle! You are **too** kind." Camilla flushed with pleasure but felt that to kiss her Mistress might be too forward. "Thank you—indeed thank you!"

And more was to come. As she hung her pelisse behind the kitchen door, Mister Castle emerged from his workshop looking shy. "My dear wife informs me that this is your birthday, my child. I wish you many happy years and trust this may be to your liking?" He held out a little phial of his latest perfume and Camilla gasped with delight:

"Why, Mister Castle, this is the most wonderful gift I have ever had! I—I do not deserve it." Her shining gray eyes met his faded ones and he nodded, smiling.

"I warrant you do, my dear. 'Tis seldom my perfume is worn by such a beautiful young lady—indeed, you have become like a daughter here." This effusion embarrassed him so much that he had almost retreated through the door before Camilla cried:

"Thank you with all my heart!" She stowed her new treasures carefully into the little reticule from mama and felt, for the first time, that at last she was truly grown up even though there could be no grand balls or parties to celebrate the momentous fact but some day, her heart sang softly. Yes, some day she might actually meet her dream lord in Curzon Street for she knew she could marry no other.

The day progressed happily—all the customers happened to be ladies and gentlemen that she liked and many had recently taken to calling her by name: Miss Camilla which was most flattering.

She went on two errands and lingered a few moments at the corner of Curzon Street but the house remained still and quiet with no waiting carriage outside. But just to have stood close to it was enough on such a gladsome day.

As a final treat Mistress Castle allowed her to go home half an hour earlier than usual. "No doubt your mama will have some small celebration waiting for you, my dear. There will be few customers at this hour and I can manage easily, I swear," Mistress Castle reassured her.

So, with renewed thanks to them both, Camilla donned

her bonnet and pelisse, took her reticule, and started on her homeward way. She should reach the tavern soon after eight o'clock and so be able to give extra help to her mother. Suddenly she had an idea—much as she longed to keep it for herself, she would give the phial of perfume to her dear, generous mother who always did so much for her, including earning the extra two shillings a week by sewing late so that Thomas Fernaby could not grumble. *Mama would never use the expensive stuff, of course,* she thought, *but would treasure it all her life for its sheer beauty.*

As she turned into Cheapside, Camilla paused, surprised. There were many more carriages outside The Crown than was usual and the windows of the first floor were aflicker with candles. What could be happening? For, as she drew nearer, she could hear much laughter and singing floating out into the gathering dusk. For one moment she wondered whether, after all, she was to have a birthday party. But this she quickly dismissed: Thomas Fernaby would never permit such an extravagance. There must be important gentlemen travelling who had sought lodgings for the night.

She slipped around the side of the tavern, through the yard and back door. Mrs. Fernaby was tired, flushed and obviously very put-about. She turned quickly as Camilla came in, almost as though she were not welcome.

"Why, Camilla! You are early I declare, I—I was not expecting ye for half an hour or more."

Camilla went straightway to hug her, and added, "Dearest Mama, Mistress Castle allowed me to leave early for they *knew* it was my birthday and oh, it has been glorious —so very happy. They even gave me gifts, and one is for you." She opened her reticule and held out the phial, resting it on the palm of her hand so that the candlelight should show the full glory of the blue Bristol glass and tiny silver stopper.

Her mother drew back hastily. "No, no, dearest child, 'tis the kindliest thought I have ever received, but such a

39

thing is not for the likes of me! Pray *you* keep it, for you are becoming a real lady these days as I trow you should be."

Camilla felt deeply disturbed—something was sadly wrong and her mother was protecting her from it as she had always done from unpleasantness. She looked at her mother gravely, but her gaze was too direct and Mrs. Fernaby shifted her own eyes and turned to fuss over a pot that had started to bubble.

Camilla went behind her and placed her hands on her mama's shoulders and turned her mother gently around to face her again.

"What is it, Mama? You are sore distressed, I vow, and I am no longer a child. Pray tell me the cause of all the lights and noise from upstairs—have we grand lodgers? And are they demanding too much work from you?"

Mrs. Fernaby had spent all day rehearsing what explanation she might offer to Camilla. Her distress at the wicked opening of the bordello added to her own burden of guilt: but for her own selfishness, her longing to keep the beloved daughter just over her birthday, the girl should have been safely boarded with the Castles before this fateful night. However the damage was done though Camilla must never know the truth. With a brave smile Mrs. Fernaby explained:

"Tis a new-fangled whim of your father's to earn more money from the smart young gentlemen who patronize The Crown. It seems one of them informed him a few days past that journeying to Cheapside for glasses of wine was becoming a bore—he declared that parties were all the thing nowadays, parties where they might entertain young ladies if they wished and enjoy a little music, too. So *that* is the new use for the rooms upstairs."

Camilla cried, "Oh, *why* did you not tell me immediately, Mama? Why, you must have toiled many hours to make those dingy rooms fit for such junketings! You, who work so hard—I would have helped you or, better still,

40

done them out for you, for I am strong and do not tire easily." She was extremely upset.

Mrs. Fernaby shook her head. "No, lovey, thanks be to the good Lord in Heaven, your way lies among the gentry now and 'tis what I have always wished and striven for. The life in a tavern is not for you—now don your apron and get busy on these fillings, for I've a fresh batch of pastry ready for rolling."

Still far from satisfied, Camilla did as she was bid. Fortunately, among the hiss and bubble of the kitchen they could no longer hear the roistering from upstairs and, having no knowledge of a bordello, she had not the slightest suspicion of what was really happening.

When the latest batch of pastries was in the oven, Thomas Fernaby shouted down the stairs, "The large jar of grog, Hannah, and make haste about it. Or no, if the girl is back make *her* bring it up!"

Mother and daughter stared at each other, their mutual fear undisguised: was Fernaby planning to drag her, after all, into his felonious plan, wondered Hannah. Whereas Camilla only dreaded being forced into the tavern against her will to serve wine and ale to the customers.

Swiftly she moved to the stone jars standing by the range to warm. Grog was made early in the evening, then simmered on the hob with an iron ladle close by to put it into the jars without waste. As she filled the largest size she said:

"Pray, *pray* do not be upset, Mama, for I declare Father cannot force me to serve it, nor shall he. There is far too much to do down here."

With more assurance than she felt, she lifted the heavy jar and carried it up the stairs in her strong young arms.

Between the kitchen stairs and the actual entry to the tavern hung a heavy baize curtain. A short passage divided the two with the staircase to the first floor leading up on the right and, again, the noise of merriment struck her ears and she paused. There was something coarse about

41

it, especially the laughter of the women. It was the kind of laughter Camilla often heard here, in the East End, but not such as made by young ladies.

However, before she could think further, the green baize curtain was drawn roughly aside and, expecting the burly figure of her father to appear she held out the jar at arms length, ready to turn and hurry back down the stairs as soon as he took it from her.

But no burly man appeared; instead an exceptionally tall, thin young man with fair hair who had become a little unruly lurched from the tavern. The dimness of the passage made him pause a moment after the bright lights he had left and he swayed on his feet. Then, as his eyes accustomed themselves, he saw Camilla apparently offering him a great jar of delicious-smelling grog. Eagerly he reached out for it, only, so uncertain were his steps, that instead he staggered forward, knocked the jar to the ground where it scattered into chunks and slivers of earthenware, while the powerful aroma of spilled grog almost overcame Camilla who stepped back against the wall.

It was not to be. Having lost the grog the young man reached out greedily for the girl who, although somewhat blurred to his vision, struck him as unusually pretty and, before she could move, he had her pinioned by the arms.

"Pray unhand me, sir," she gasped, bending her head back against the wall, sickened by the stench of wine on his breath allied to the grog. But he only laughed thickly in his throat.

"Coy, eh?" He pulled her roughly forward so that his arms encircled her slender waist and then drew her lovely face close in an attempt to focus.

"By gad, I sh–shwear ye're a beauty, me lass!" He attempted to bend down and kiss her but only succeeded in taking two uncertain steps backwards which led them both into the pink light thrown down from the candle sconces fixed on the wall of the stairs.

"Like a bit o' coq–coquetry—stap me, all thish for a

guinea!" He tried a hearty laugh which ended in a choking cough. Sir Caspar Randal was very drunk indeed.

Meantime, Camilla had summoned up her courage and said coldly, "I am daughter to Thomas Fernaby, owner of The Crown. I demand that you release me *this instant!*"

Her command either went unheard or was deliberately misunderstood as his hot, clammy hands increased their pressure around her waist.

"Never thought 'twould be sho dec–deschent here! Stap me, no! You musht be the Peach in ol' Ma Fernaby's dish! And I'll have you, by my life I'll have you *now!* Help me up the dam' shtairs, girl, gi' a hand, eh?"

As he forced her to the lowest step Camilla took her greatest risk. With all the breath at her command after Sir Caspar's relentless grip on her waist, she called,

"Father—Father, pray come!"

She scarce heard the baize curtain move for her head was whirling—whirling with the shock and the appalling speculation which his drunken words had set up in her mind. In a stumbling, lurching way he had turned her to face the stairs so that his back was toward the tavern and he was oblivious to sound by then.

Suddenly, as she was near to swooning with fear and disgust, her persecutor was torn away from her and she found she could breathe. A deep, resonant voice said, "I declare you're drunk again, Randal—let the wench go! Did you not hear her call for her father?" Strong, dark hands pushed him half up the stairs. "Go to your filthy pleasures if you must! For myself, I would not take one step in that direction!"

Scrambling and cursing, the fair man called Randal went, spider-fashion, to the first floor, grumbling, "Where ish my Peach? Damme, Monford, ye want her for yerself."

"I believe her to be Thomas Fernaby's daughter and you will leave her alone! You've ruined the jar she was carrying, I see, that's enough out of you!"

Camilla had shrunk back against the wall. Now her rescuer turned to her with a slight, apologetic smile.

"Alas, I fear Sir Caspar Randal is well into his cups—he is never a man to my taste, so call to your father if you should encounter him again. I rarely frequent inns myself."

Camilla gasped: he was her Lord of Curzon Street!

Her eyes grew wide and dark with wonderment—then shame flooded her cheeks with color: that she should meet him here, of all places, in the dim passageway of a tavern and her apron splashed and stained with grog! Little more than a servant and a humble one at that.

Without waiting for her thanks or even a reply, he went down on one immaculate, silken knee and began to gather the shards of earthenware together. Covered with confusion Camilla cried:

"Oh, my lord, pray, *pray* do not demean yourself so! Your elegant hose . . . !" Swiftly she sank on her knees beside him, her own hands working feverishly to clear the pieces. He looked up and smiled, his face more devastating than ever.

"I am no 'lord,' I fear—only Sir Michael Monford at your service. As to my hose, be dammed to that! I was about to drive home in any case, only your father was eager that we should all wait to let him present his beautiful daughter." He looked at her more closely. "And by my troth you have a charming face, Miss Fernaby."

It was a kindly compliment, casually spoken, but being enamored as she was, Camilla felt unjustly hurt for the word "beauty" could never apply to a wench from Cheapside, only to the gracious young ladies who inhabited his own world. Bravely she managed a smile.

"Thank you, sir—now I beg you to rise for you have helped me much. I will fetch a pail and have the passage cleaned in no time."

He laughed, a pleasant sound. "Never spurn willing aid —to tell the truth I find it more diverting to be of use here than lounging in a tavern. Perhaps that is unpardonable since your father owns The Crown!"

Throwing caution to the winds for she would certainly

never meet him again, Camilla managed a small laugh.

"In truth I, too, dislike the tavern—my father wants me to serve there but I will not. I prefer to help my mother with her cooking." Emboldened she went further, since he was still smiling and the shards lay neatly gathered between them. "Perchance you are a man of action, Sir Michael? Riding and such."

His face lightened still further and, for a moment he forgot her humble status.

"Ah, now that is grand sport, I declare! Indeed, I have a likely gelding for the races at Brighton this summer when His Royal Highness is in residence at the Royal Pavilion. But I beg your forgiveness for my enthusiasm—naturally you can have no interest in horses!"

"I do not ride, no, but I find horses beautiful to watch." She longed to tell him that she saw many fine animals in the West End and in Curzon Street itself, but then changed her mind. It was bad enough to be an Innkeeper's daughter in Cheapside, but if she added that she worked in a shop, however fashionable by day, it would not raise his opinion of her at all. They were from different worlds and it was a gap that could not be bridged.

"You have a gentle voice, Miss Fernaby. 'Twould soothe any animal I declare." He stood up and Camilla did the same, glancing with horror at the grog stain on his knee.

"Oh, sir—would that I might wash your silk stockings for you—once dry that mark will not be removed I fear."

He glanced down, laughing, then looked at his own sorry state. "Thank you, but a pair of hose is nothing to me I assure you—much better wash your own garments, I declare!"

Suddenly the baize curtain was pulled roughly aside and Thomas Fernaby stood glaring at them. With dread, Camilla saw that his face was more deeply flushed than usual since he had shared in many toasts to the success of The Crown Bordello that evening.

"Ha!" he sneered at Sir Michael. "Tried to steal me

45

good wares wi'out payin' eh? Well let me tell *you*, me fine gentleman, the girls workin' fer me cost a sovereign a time"—he grew truculent—"Seein' yer've had yer fun ye'll pay up or I'll call the Watch!"

Camilla stepped forward, white to the lips.

"How dare you speak so, Father? This gentleman was kindly . . ."

"Hold yer tongue, girl—I'll deal wi' ye later. Get up the stairs and earn yer keep along o' the other wenches now I know ye're no better'n yer should be!"

Sir Michael's face had turned to granite. The wench was a doxy after all who had made mock of him. How Caspar Randal would laugh when she regaled him with such a tale! Without a word he drew out his purse and flung, first, a sovereign at her then another to Thomas Fernaby who chuckled lewdly.

The young man never heard Camilla's inarticulate cry as he strode proudly away, pushing past the landlord who stumbled in astonishment, and straight out of the tavern door.

She could not trust herself to speak for she knew that anger, chagrin, and bitter hurt would combine at any moment into a flood of helpless tears. With the toe of her slipper she kicked with disdain the sovereign thrown to her toward her hateful father and turned away as he picked up both coins greedily.

Camilla turned away as he returned to the tavern, grumbling, for she could feel her heart breaking in her breast like a helpless creature in torment. Never, never again would she see her noble hero. She must not even indulge the simple pleasure of watching to catch a glimpse of him in Curzon Street, for the scorn in his eyes should he remember her would be beyond all endurance.

With tears blinding her she fetched a pail from the small broom closet by the kitchen stairs and gathered up the shards. Then, unable to stem the sobs that wracked her any longer she stumbled down the stairs and straight into Mrs. Fernaby's anxious arms.

46

"Oh, my little love, what has happened?" she cried as Camilla clung to her fiercely, her face buried against her mother's comforting shoulder. Never had Mrs. Fernaby heard such heartbroken weeping and the girl was obviously beyond answering any questions for the time being. Tenderly she stroked the beautiful, silky hair, crooning gentle, soft sounds as she might to a hurt child.

But, over Camilla's bowed head, her eyes grew bleak and frightened as her kindly mouth hardened. What had Thomas done to the girl to transform her from the shining, carefree figure that had come in scarce two hours since?

At that moment Fernaby himself appeared at the top of the stairs, his bloodshot eyes taking in the scene with increasing fury. "Stop cossetting that wicked wench, Hannah!" he growled. "She's not above kissin' and cuddlin' some fine gentleman on the sly in a dark passage, oh, no! Ye'll order her up to the first floor this minute or 'twill go ill with both o' ye!"

A great shudder shook Camilla's slight frame and Hannah Fernaby held her more closely. "Ye're an evil man, husband. Get back to yer duties—*if* ye can walk that far for the drink inside ye! The child is ill and ye'll not touch her!" The fuddled man was taken aback, he had never heard such hatred in his wife's tone and momentarily it sobered him a little.

He hesitated then delivered his parting shot before leaving them alone. "Connivin', eh? Well, we'll see who's master here—just ye wait!"

The welcome silence weighed on both mother and daughter for Camilla's tears had ceased at his cruel words and the older woman was frightened although she attempted to hide it. Could she take Camilla back to the Castles immediately? But a glance at the kitchen told her it was impossible at such a late hour.

Slowly Camilla drew herself up straight again and gently stepped back to clasp her mother's hands. "Dear, dear Mama—he shall not harm you I swear—and—and I was *not* behaving wantonly with Sir Michael! Indeed he is the most chivalrous young gentleman I ever met. I declare he was helping me in the passageway to gather up pieces of the grog jar broken by a hateful young man who tried to kiss me." She hesitated, not wanting to distress her mother further, but the words were forced out of her through the ache in her heart. "And Mr. Fernaby—for *never* will I call him 'Father' again—insulted him beyond bearing. I have never felt so shamed . . ."

Mrs. Fernaby had summoned all her self-control that her lined face showed no more trace of her inner fear. "I know you would never do anything wicked, daughter, and have no fears on my account—ye're father will be too drunk to remember what has passed, I swear. Now, don't try to talk about it yet; sit you down and I'll brew up a good pot o' tea; I'm thinkin' we could both do with some."

She turned to busy herself with the kettle and a battered pewter teapot while Camilla automatically fetched cups and saucers to the table. Both were too preoccupied with their thoughts to talk frankly. For the first time the girl was longing to tell her mother everything—of her foolish dreams of belonging in the West End, her watching for Sir Michael on the corner of Curzon Street, and the miracle of meeting him tonight which now had ruined all her future hopes . . . .

But Mrs. Fernaby's thoughts were very different: a desolate sense of loss for, by morning, Camilla would know the whole truth of her birth and would, most justly, turn against her foster-mother forever.

The tea was strong and reviving, yet both said nothing. At last Mrs. Fernaby spoke tentatively: "You speak of this Sir Michael most warmly, my dear—is he a customer at the shop?"

"No—and now I pray that he never will be for should he recognize me I fear I should die of shame! Why, Mistress Castle should surely turn me out if he does!" The thought shocked her and her gray eyes darkened. "He—

he was a dream, Mama, a foolish childish dream, you see . . ."

Slowly Camilla told her mother of the precious moments in Curzon Street, ending: "I knew 'twould never be —that I could never meet him for, while many of the young noblemen are grand and even pleasant, Sir Michael is grand in a *different* way."

"And you are in love with him, child."

"Yes—and more so than ever after this evening for he is so kind and charming"—Camilla's voice hardened—"but after such an ugly scene I must forget him, I *must*. I declare, if I were presented to him as a princess he would still regard me as a loose woman, a—a *harlot* such as Mr. Fernaby implied. Oh, Mama, he is a wicked, wicked old man—I swear I will work night as well as day to take you from here!"

Her mother's eyes were warm but infinitely sad. "That can never be, my Camilla, but for you the way ahead will be very different, I declare." She stood up. "Come, let us clear this kitchen for we cannot talk until your father— until my *husband*," she corrected herself quickly, "has departed up to bed for then we shall be undisturbed."

As Camilla rolled up her sleeves and washed glasses and dishes at the smaller sink, her mother scoured baking tins, pots, and utensils at the big one with unusual vigor. She even went over one or two again, although they were spotless—anything to put off the moment when Camilla would face her with questions in her eyes.

It was nearly closing time and the roisterers from upstairs were straggling down and along the passage, screams of laughter floating down the stairs. Camilla listened intently and, when one of the girls shouted a coarse remark, she could have sworn she recognized the voice from somewhere in the neighborhood.

One look at her mother's set face and she remained silent. All in good time she would learn the truth and, meantime, she forced her thoughts to remain wistfully on

Sir Michael's face, his smile that showed such white teeth, the warmth in his dark eyes and the long, tapering fingers that had gathered shards so adroitly. Oh, *if only*—yet "if only" what? Her glorious dreams of living a fairy tale, of being transported by magic into the elegant, wealthy world of the *ton* lay in shreds. After tonight she knew that there was no magic, for she had been born into a lowly estate and they had not. Nothing, not even the care mama had taken over the years to make her speak as they did with no trace of a cockney accent, could change or hide the stark facts. She sighed.

Mrs. Fernaby went to the foot of the stairs and listened intently for a few moments, then she turned back.

"Well," she said flatly, "he's abiding by the law at least! The tavern doors must be closed for there are but two or three voices up there now." Bitterness crept into her tone. "Some rich wine-bibbers, no doubt, with plenty of gold in their purses to whom he has granted the *favor* of staying behind to talk with him. As if he weren't too drunk already to speak plain! Ah well, I warrant he'll be carousing 'till the early hours or more."

She was talking to lengthen the time before she knew she must make her revelations and Camilla, understanding this, felt a strange unease. What more, on this most tragic of evenings, was about to beset her?

Her mother indicated a kitchen chair and then placed herself on the one opposite. For a long, perhaps last, moment her eyes dwelt lovingly on the beautiful girl she might never see again.

"Camilla, my dearest daughter, this grieves me beyond measure. But it is your right, now that you are turned eighteen, to learn the truth. Oh, I would have told you in any case, but I was selfish, afeared to lose the one joy of my life."

Camilla's gray eyes widened. "But, Mama, how *could* you lose me? Whatever you have to say you are my *mother*, the one I care for most in all the world!" Shock had even driven out the memory of Sir Michael momentarily.

Mrs. Fernaby paused, her hands clenched tightly on her lap. Then, keeping her voice firm, she began: "You said, Camilla, that even were Sir Michael to be presented to you as a princess he would always consider you . . . a loose woman."

"Indeed yes, since he studied my face closely." Yet, as she spoke, Camilla's heart began throbbing with excitement—was this, after all, to take a fairy tale twist?

Mrs. Fernaby shook her head: "With all my heart, lovey, I would make you a princess if I could but that, I fear, cannot be." Her little smile was rueful. "I declare, I would give you the crown of England if 'twould help you, but that I cannot do. But you are not base-born—you are a born aristocrat, child, you belong up there in the West End among the grand folk."

" 'Tis not *possible!*" gasped the girl, her eyes glowing.

"You are a French countess in your own right, Camilla, descended from a long line of grand gentry!"

Chapter Four

A *Countess!* How could such a dazzling fact be possible? While her whole being pulsated at the words, Camilla was deeply loyal, and concern for her mother, now looking so weary and sad, overcame all else. She slipped from her chair and sat on the floor by her mother's knee as she had done so often through the years.

"Dearest Mama, I beg you to tell me the whole story but have no fear. If I am truly high born, 'twill be a miracle, but how could it separate me from you? Why, it increases my love and hopes beyond belief since it may give me the means to save you from this—this truly terrible life!"

Mrs. Fernaby's heart welled with thankfulness, yet she said, "Wait, my love, for there is more to tell—much more."

Camilla looked up at her trustingly: "Pray tell me everything for it must have been a sore burden to add to the many others."

Quietly, Mrs. Fernaby told of her birth and her beautiful young mother, but she was forced to add:

"She and your poor father had only escaped from France with their lives and, when he died, not one penny piece had they left between them, poor souls. Oh, I pressed your dear mother for any names of kith and kin— any French friends who might have helped them and to whom you could be entrusted—but she knew of none such by name. They had come to seek, she told me, having lost all the grand estates and fortune of the family to them dammed revolutionaries . . ."

"What was her name?" asked Camilla gently.

"The name that is yours now, Camilla—Countess de Courville. She declared it to be yours by right, tho' I know not how for I confess I know little of such grand matters."

"Countess de Courville," murmured Camilla, finding it pleasing beyond belief in spite of the lack of any fortune to match such grace and grandeur. She was young and spirited and, somehow, she would find those whom her tragic young parents had come to seek out.

Meantime Mrs. Fernaby, launching into a full confession, went on:

"How could I hide the truth from my husband once he heard ye crying?" Her smile was rueful. "For ye had such a powerful pair o' lungs, my love, and Thomas would have needed to be deaf as a post not to hear those cries when ye were hungry!"

"Did he object?"

Her mother sighed: "Aye, indeed he did! Had ye been a son he'd have been different, I warrant; but a girl, in his eyes, meant only another drudge, a servant not a pair o' sturdy arms to work with him!"

"Did he know that I was a countess?"

Mrs. Fernaby sighed: "At first, yes. He had great hopes of a rich reward, I fancy. But when he learned that I knew not where to look for your friends or kin he turned surly . . ."

"So *that* is why he resents me so! Oh, Mama, pray tell me all of it—all—I would know everything that has occurred since my birth!"

In her heart Camilla had already resolved to scour England in search of any person who had known the de Courvilles, but above all she wished to relieve the obvious guilt felt by the kindly woman who had come to mean all the world to her.

"Well—at first Thomas was all for sending you off to the Poorhouse"—her mother's voice hardened—"and you but a tiny, helpless mite! From that day on I vowed to keep you since *he* never gave me one of my own to hold in my arms!"

Camilla reached up and took the work-worn hands in her own:

"Oh, dearest Mama—what you have suffered for me! When I find the de Courvilles—for find them I will, I swear—then shall you have the reward and, by my life, I shall love you 'til I die!"

Hannah Fernaby wiped her eyes, quite overcome by such deep affection that she had feared would turn to loathing:

"*You* have been my reward, Camilla—indeed, I need no other," she declared, holding the slender hands more fervently.

Camilla's mind was working furiously since the whole of her future life now seemed so very different to anything she had even dreamed of. It never occurred to her that her search for some distant relatives might fail. But one immediate relief was uppermost in her mind.

"Oh, Mama! How truly thankful I am to learn that, indeed, Thomas Fernaby is not my true father! It has tormented me that I should fear him as I do—so sinful!"

Mrs. Fernaby's face hardened again:

" 'Twas no sin, my child it—"

Eagerly Camilla interrupted the sentence: "But now that I know the truth life here will be very different, I swear! Why, if he pesters me again to serve the ale and wine, I shall *behave* like a Countess"—a little laugh of delight rippled in her voice—"I might even become haughty and call him 'My man!' in a tone the duchess uses on occasion in our shop!"

The moment Hannah Fernaby had dreaded most of all had come.

"Camilla, I fear that you will have no such chance. For, alas, you must bide here no longer." The girl looked up, startled, as her mother hastened on: "I fear that only my selfishness—*my* sin—has kept you with me 'til now. I—I wished with all my heart to see your eighteenth birthday else I would have asked Mistress Castle to take you into her keeping long since."

"Leave *here?* Oh, Mama, pray do not send me away now! Do you not see that what you have told me changes everything? That he can no longer give me orders? And I can protect you . . . at least, a little."

"A title is very splendid, dear child, but without money it gives you no power. Thomas is, indeed, an evil man but he speaks true when he declares that you owe him much over these years and now he has a most shocking way to force you to repay him."

Camilla looked up in puzzlement, so her mother went on, forcing out the dreadful words that offended her very soul:

"I lied to you this evening, Camilla—the only lie I ever told you in all your life. Those parties on the first floor . . ." her voice failed her at such horror but, with a deep breath she pressed on: "They are no such thing. No, tonight, 'gainst all my protests, my husband opened what he boasts of as The Crown Bordello." Camilla gave a horrified gasp although she had part guessed already. In a harsh tone Mrs. Fernaby spelled out the fact as if to add to her own torture: "Here, under our own roof, there is a bawdy house—a shameful place where women of the street are to ply their hateful trade while Thomas gathers in the gold!"

Camilla's first reaction shamed her for it was purely selfish: Sir Michael Monford! No wonder his chivalrous, fine nature had spurned her with such scorn. As her broken hearted pain returned, she wholly understood his attitude—knew that, no matter what revelations of her rank she might discover, he would regard her forever as a loose woman, a harlot . . . .

Nervous now, Mrs. Fernaby hurried on: "My husband's determination is that you should be one of those—those

55

sinful creatures and, if I die first, I would protect you my dearest one. That is why you must beg Mistress Castle to take you in on the morrow and never, never come to The Crown again!" Silent tears streamed down her lined, tired face and Camilla, shocked by her own instinctive selfishness, slipped a protective arm around her mother's thin shoulders, her mind racing once more:

"Pray, oh, pray do not weep, Mama—'twill break my heart to leave you, but I swear it shall be only for a little while."

Slowly, Mrs. Fernaby collected herself. "Before you depart," she said, "I have a packet that I promised your mother I would hold for you. I do not know what it contains for it bears your name on the front and I have resolved should only be opened by you when you were of age. I have hidden it all these years from my husband—in case it contained money—in my straw hat that I wear for funerals, drawn down by black veiling to semble a bonnet—for black bonnets are only for widows!"

With supreme self-control, for her urgency now drove her mercilessly, Camilla cried:

"Pray, Mama, fetch it this instant—he is still in the tavern and you may have at least some minutes before he seeks his bed."

The older woman darted out of the kitchen door to the outside stairway in spite of a whirling head and legs almost too leaden to climb. In the kitchen Camilla stood tense, feeling her life to be in the balance; if Mr. Fernaby lurched in she determined to hold him in conversation, hard though it would prove. Yet, at last, she knew that she was no longer his daughter—his power over her was gone and her inner hatred could have free rein.

Seconds later Mrs. Fernaby returned, her funeral straw in her hand, her eyes kindling:

" 'Tis here, Camilla, but I confess I have not the strength to tear out the lining, should it be a sad disappointment."

56

Camilla took the hat, her hands trembling.

She picked up the kitchen scissors and, most carefully, began to unpick the lining for, even in her excitement, she would not spoil mama's funeral hat.

Watching her, Mrs. Fernaby held her breath until, at last, Camilla drew out a large vellum envelope, yellowed by the years. They both stared at it, agog to see the contents yet fearful of finding out.

At last, with a quick movement, Camilla broke the ancient seal and drew out the contents which numbered three items. The first proved to be a half-sheet penned by her late mother in a shaky hand and halting English:

> *Dearest Child—boy or girl I not yet know. Papa and I love you much. He help pen this in English avec me, for English you will be. Yet de Courville you are—proud name en France. Hélas, we have nothing to give but such proud a name and beauty a little, we think. Seek, dearest petit or petite for such may come. Love is all we have and is yours—all yours.*

> *Mama*

Tears misted Camilla's lovely eyes as she passed this sad heritage of love to Mrs. Fernaby who, after scanning it, wept with her:

"Oh, lovey, she was indeed beautiful—and gentle as you are I declare. Your poor papa had died when she reached me and the humble refuge I could offer, but I warrant he was young and handsome too."

Camilla would not hurt her for the world, yet knew she wished to read the other contents in private. Suddenly the proud blood of centuries coursed through her veins and, if disappointment lay ahead she preferred to face it alone. Wiping her tears aside she looked across at mama. "I know they are jealously guarded by Mr. Fernaby but —could I take a tallow candle up to my room, Mama?" she asked hesitantly. "I swear that I have been most careful of the one he allows me each week but 'tis burnt to scarce high enough to see my way to bed now and I—I would study the other papers with care."

Thankful that she had properly executed her duty to the late young countess after all, Mrs. Fernaby went to the jar and took out two candles, handing them lovingly to Camilla. "There, my dearest child, I thank the good Lord that He has seen fit to give you proof of your nobility—should my husband count the candles, I shall gladly declare that one was for myself." They stood facing each other, the moment almost too charged with emotion.

Then Camilla took the older woman tenderly in her embrace. "Mama, nothing can ever change the love I bear you—I swear it. And should good fortune attend my search, I vow to save you from this place—this life of cruel drudgery."

Then, carrying the two precious candles carefully with the remaining pages to be devoured, she went out and climbed the stairs to her attic room for the last time.

In order to be absolutely secure in her privacy, Camilla did not light a candle immediately. Instead, she lay, fully clothed on top of her coverlet, staring wide-eyed into the darkness until the heavy, uncertain steps of Thomas Fernaby wove into the next-door attic and a heaving and creaking announced his collapse into bed.

Even then Camilla was loth to light a candle. Sleep had never been further from her—for what a dramatic change her eighteenth birthday had brought to her life: first, the meeting with the man of her dreams, Sir Michael and, later, the miraculous knowledge that her vivid dreams of belonging to the *haute monde* were no fairy tale imaginings. She was an aristocrat, bearing a high title that might place her in the forefront of society.

At long last, when the tavern house was silent save for Fernaby's stentorous snores, she lit a candle and drew out the papers still unread from the old envelope.

At first the fear of disillusion was as powerful as her thirst for more knowledge—more proof. But, choosing the single vellum sheet penned in English her spirits rose. It was a legal document, signed and sealed by a French man of law, although his English was far from perfect but, studying the date and considering her own age, Camilla knew it must have been written shortly before her parents left France for England. And it was unmistakably addressed to any English Court who disputed their claims to the de Courville titles and restoration of their estates.

Eagerly she pored over it, finding the formal phraseology hard to understand at first. Yet one paragraph stood out in letters of fire:

> The child due to be born to the Count and Countess de Courville, be it male or female, shall hold the family title in his or her own right for all time. This has been decreed by our most gracious and blessed King, Louis XVI, who has been pleased to grant the title in perpetuity for extreme bravery by the first Count Henri de Courville.

Camilla sat back on her bed, holding the precious paper as reverently as she might have held the Holy Grail. It was unheard of for a woman to inherit a noble title in her own right at that time, yet the courage of her grandfather must have been such that it inspired a breaking of tradition by his king.

In no hurry now to scan the final paper she closed her eyes and tried, in vain, to imagine her grandfather—that he must have been extremely handsome she accepted, but had he ridden forth alone, in full armour and a plumed helmet to accost the enemy? Or, in elegant court dress, thwarted all the king's enemies by his skill in diplomacy?

His image refused to be conjured up but, with heartfelt admiration, his grand-daughter saluted him in her humble attic. She was a true countess as a result of his actions and, humbly, she thanked him.

Lastly she came to a letter that frustrated her eager

59

searching for further knowledge of the past. It was entirely written in French and worse, the scratchy writing went not only down the page but then across it as was the habit of the time.

"It is my own language," murmured Camilla in vexation, "yet I know not one word!"

Only two things were clear—the bold signature: Claudette de Courville, and, half-way down the second page a name and address printed in capitals. It was only a straw but the girl clung to it, returning to it again and again as if it had some mystic message to reveal:

Le Marquis de Fouchet,
Chateau Fouchet,
Bois de Boulogne,
Paris.

At last, despondently, she almost gave up—'twas most likely the address of some friend of the old lady, or even the correct address where some grand ball was to be held. Then her eyes strayed to the sentence immediately after: *"Il vous aidera toujours, Cherie."*

Her ardent hope revived a little; surely "aidez" *must* mean "aid" as it did in English. The letter itself was very old—older than herself, by the date, and the ink had faded a great deal. It was possible that this Marquis de Fouchet was no longer alive and, if he were, he could hardly be living in a grand house in Paris after the revolution? But it was all she had to go on at present since the lawyer's signature at the foot of her precious deed of entitlement was an illegible scrawl underlined by a flourish.

Youth was on her side and Camilla's spirit rose from renewed hope to definite expectation: she would write to this Marquis, for, even had he died, he would surely have relatives still living—relatives who must know something of the great de Courville family?

Her mind was so filled with a glowing, if distant, future that she forgot that on the morrow she must be parted from her beloved mama and her home . . . .

She could not sleep but lay down, the precious papers held close against her breast, and allowed her imagination to run free.

Mrs. Fernaby could not sleep either, for her weary heart was torn in two—anguish at being forced to send Camilla away and yet, thankfulness that the beautiful girl might, at last, come into her own.

Finally, driven mad by the heavy snores of her husband, she rose stealthily, donned her many petticoats and blouse, then stole from the attic, closing the latch with her breath held so that it would give no tell-tale "click."

In the kitchen the embers of last night's fire still glowed faintly red and, with added fuel, were soon coaxed back into flame. Then, lighting yet another tallow candle, she took a piece of cheap, rough paper from the dresser drawer (kept for making out bills for overnight travelling lodgers), a quill pen, and a bottle of ink.

Mrs. Fernaby had learnt to read, painstakingly, from her uncle who owned a prosperous pawn brokers business in Holborn when Camilla was still a baby, for the child must be taught the skill as she grew older. But writing did not come easily since she had little practice. At last she began:

Dear Thomasina,
I pray of your good heart that you will take in my daughter, Camilla, to bed and board in your house from this very day.
She is now in danger here.
                              Your true friend,
                              Hannah Fernaby

When she was satisfied that the spelling was correct she heard a light step outside and Camilla came in, surprised to find her mother up even before dawn:

"Why, Mama, could you not sleep either? I will put the kettle to boil . . ."

"I have penned a note for you to take to Mistress Castle, child, for you cannot ask for shelter without explanation." Mrs. Fernaby's gaze rested sadly, lovingly, on the beloved face but she was resolved to make the moment no harder with emotion. "I will go up, now, and fetch your few things so we can bundle them into a shawl since we have nothing grander."

Suddenly, the immediate future overcame Camilla's golden thoughts of the future and she held out her hands in pleading:

"Need I truly leave you, Mama—now that Mr. Fernaby will not dare to touch me since I have a title and nothing is hid any longer? I would stay with you, *indeed* I would!"

Hannah Fernaby shook her head. " 'Tis not possible, dear child. That man is a master of trickery and will stop at nothing. Nay, you brew the tea while I fetch the clothes," she instructed. "They are poor enough, in all conscience, for a grand countess! Have you those papers safe?"

Eyes glowing again, Camilla touched the bosom of her dress.

"They are close to my heart, Mama, and always will be. Why, there is even a grand gentleman, a Marquis, to whom I mean to write! Oh, all will come right, I swear it!"

Mrs. Fernaby slipped out and climbed the attic stairs with a heavy heart: Camilla had already left her care in spirit and 'twas only right that she should do so, but the wrench was sore hard to bear. Thomas Fernaby's snores had grown louder and made enough noise for her purpose as she moved swiftly around the smaller attic, gathering up each trace of her daughter's occupation.

Alone in the kitchen, waiting for the kettle to bubble, Camilla found her dreams too strong to resist, sad though she was for her mother. She *had* to pin all her faith in a reply from the Marquis since she held no other clue to the past. But then . . . oh, then she would surely meet Sir Michael again at some grand ball or dinner party for the elite. She would be transformed from the humble servant at a tavern into a beautifully gowned, bejewelled countess, schooled in the wit and delicate manners of society to win his heart—or, at least, his attention. For how could he possibly associate her with such a sordid background?

That her blazing hope, the old Marquis, might not respond, she refused to admit in her heart. Had she not always known, sensed that she *belonged* to the *haute monde?* She had many flights of imagination, many dreams but this one *was* based in truth.

Mrs. Fernaby returned and together they folded the few dresses and spotless underwear, all lovingly made by Hannah herself, along with hair ribbons, a bone comb, and the few fal-las collected over the years and soon all was ready to take. The blue gowns that Mistress Castle had commissioned for Camilla to wear in the shop were jealously kept there for fear of misuse and, each morning, a fresh one hung on the kitchen door for the girl to change into.

The sun had just risen and the day bid fair so Camilla said:

"I shall wrap them in my pelisse, Mama, for it is pretty and will not resemble the crude bundle of a travelling vagrant—I shall walk fast and feel no morning chill."

So it was arranged and, with her bonnet and little reticule laid ready, Camilla already felt all her past links with The Crown loosening—save those that bound her to mama.

"You will not leave on an empty stomach, my child," said Mrs. Fernaby briskly, holding her grief at bay. "See, I have set two leftovers to warm, the tea is brewed and there is plenty of good bread and dripping."

Camilla didn't feel like eating—'twas as impossible as sleep on this morning of high adventure—but she could not hurt her dear mother so, sitting dutifully at the table, she nibbled a pastry, crumbled a small piece of bread as she drank the tea gratefully, for she was thirsty.

Then the moment had come and they both rose.

Mrs. Fernaby held her arms wide and, with a small cry,

Camilla ran into their shelter for the last time, her dreams set aside in this final moment of parting:

"Oh, Mama—you will not let him harm you?" Her tears mingled with her mother's now. "I swear—indeed, I vow on my very life that I will save you . . ."

"God's blessing go with you, dearest daughter—go now, I pray, and do not look back. Your way lies forward from now on . . ." she released her embrace and opened the back door.

With a last look around the familiar kitchen, her eyes misty with tears, Camilla went, leaving The Crown and all that was safe and loving behind her forever.

When she was out of sight she paused a moment to dry her eyes and draw a deep breath. Then, squaring her slender shoulders she walked on firmly, with a touch of pride. She was alone now with but two burning goals to strengthen her through the battles ahead: to prove her title to the world and to win the love and respect of her shining prince—Sir Michael.

It was only as she drew near to the shop that apprehension dimmed her visions: supposing Mistress Castle spurned Mrs. Fernaby's plea and refused to take her in? Board and lodging would amount to much more than a shilling a week and she resented any expense.

A shiver passed over Camilla—for then she would be a homeless pauper with nowhere to turn for shelter and no one to whom she could appeal. Swiftly she pulled herself up: "I must not turn coward now," she whispered firmly. "This is but the first step toward my new life." And she walked steadily on.

She arrived earlier than usual and Mister and Mistress Castle were but just finishing breakfast when she tapped on the door. Letting her in, Mistress Castle looked none too pleased—zeal and punctuality she demanded, but this was an intrusion.

"Mercy me, what brings you here at this hour?" she asked with annoyance. "Mister Castle dislikes being disturbed at his breakfast."

"I—I'm sorry, indeed. I did not know the exact time, I fear, and I will wait here quietly in the shop without causing you trouble at all." Nervously she drew out the note: "Perchance I may give you this letter from my mother so that you may have time to consider . . ."

"Consider? And what, pray, does that mean?" Mistress Castle's eyes sharpened with suspicion.

"The—the letter will explain," said Camilla, her knees trembling in spite of her resolve to have courage.

The folded paper was almost snatched from her hand and the girl apologized defensively, "I am sorry that the paper is not of the quality used here and there is no envelope—but we had no need for such things at The Crown."

"H'm!" Neither Mistress Castle's tone nor her abrupt return to the kitchen, bearing the note between thumb and forefinger as if it were contaminated gave reassurance. She closed the door sharply behind her.

For the first time Camilla found the silence in the pretty shop oppressive. The early sun had not fulfilled its promise and the light from outside was a trifle overcast so that even the glass phials and crystal bottles lacked their usual sparkle.

Camilla sat forlornly on her worldly goods as though she no longer belonged here. Minutes ticked by cruelly on the small silver clock and only a murmuring came from the kitchen . . . would Mister Castle champion mama's brief plea for help? Or would his wife prove too strong on this occasion since the matter of board and lodging was her province.

At last, when the waiting had become well nigh unbearable, her name was called and, unsteadily, she rose to her feet dreading the moment when she must open that door . . . .

Chastened and nervous she stood just inside, hands clasped in front of her and her head a little bent. It was Mister Castle who addressed her first, his voice kindly:

"Come, come child, why so timid? Are we not your

65

friends, my dear wife and I? I understand there is trouble for you at home?"

"Oh yes, sir, I declare there *is!*" She held back the flood with difficulty, for Mistress Castle would never entertain the idea of giving her a home if she even guessed that The Crown now owned a bordello. Mister Castle left the table and went toward his pharmacy:

"Have no fear, my dear. My wife has made her decision." He left and so Camilla was forced to face Mistress Castle alone.

The small lips were pursed, the eyes still sharp as she said:

"Your mother makes great demands on an old friendship, I declare. You understand that if I grant her request much more service will be demanded from you to pay for our generosity?" Camilla nodded, not trusting herself to speak for, however harsh the bargain, she had no choice but to accept. More placidly Mistress Castle went on: "I have long thought of hiring help in the house but, if you will perform the duties of cleaning, setting, and cleaning the fires, dusting and polishing, then I will take you in. Since being turned into the street is your only choice, I feel sure you will agree? It is generous indeed."

"I agree and—thank you." Camilla managed the words of thanks with difficulty. She had no illusions of the drudgery that lay ahead. But this was only her first—and essential—step on the road she must follow and there was no turning back.

At the very first opportunity she would write to the Marquis de Fouchet and in her heart she offered a fervent prayer:

"Please, *please,* dear God, let him be still alive!"

Chapter Five

Mistress Castle so ruthlessly kept Camilla to their bargain that there was hardly time for her to appreciate the pretty little bedroom given to her, with its dainty, dimity curtains patterned with rosebuds and matching quilt on the narrow bed. Instead, by the end of each day Camilla was half asleep before her head touched the pillow, more exhausted than she had ever felt at The Crown.

But her natural resilience came to the rescue and soon she became accustomed to the drudgery as well as attending the shop. On her fifth day, the chance came she had been waiting for—to have a brief time with Mister Castle alone.

Determined to keep her title a secret for the time being, she had considered exactly what to say:

"Mister Castle, I can read and write well, as you know, but I confess I am sadly ignorant in many ways."

His gentle eyes twinkled. "I feared that my dear wife was over-taxing you, child—are you telling me you wish to take lessons as well?"

"No, no." Camilla smiled. " 'Tis not that. Only I wish to write a letter to—to someone who befriended me in childhood and who now resides in France but—but I have no writing paper nor quill and ink." She flushed charmingly at the presumption. "I pray that you may come to my aid for I would not trouble Mistress Castle."

The old man chuckled, obviously pleased. "My dear, 'tis a small request indeed," and he opened a desk drawer. "If you wish to send a love letter you had best take plenty!"

"Oh, 'tis no love letter, I swear," she exclaimed. "My friend must be a great age now, I wish to know how he fares."

"Very kind, Camilla, very kind. But may I inquire whether you understand about mailing such a letter? There will be a charge, you understand."

Her face fell. "I warrant I have been foolish not to think—of course there will be money to pay." She paused, then her face brightened. "I have it! My mother's uncle has a pawn broker's in Holborn and he is good to us. Since 'tis spring, I shall take him my pelisse and I declare he will advance me such as I require. 'Twill be but a trifling sum, I think."

Her gray eyes were so candid, her smile so genuine that Mister Castle knew that she meant exactly what she said. To ask for a sheet or two of paper was not begging, but she had had no intention to beg for the price of despatching her letter.

He patted her shoulder. "Nay, my dear—to part with your charming pelisse would surely bring inclement weather upon us! I frequently have cause to send to France, for there is a Monastery at Grasse that brews rare ingredients for perfumes. If you will entrust your letter to me I shall send it for you." He waved an airy hand to dismiss her blushing protests. "Say no more—you have brought new life to this house and this small service in return gives me much pleasure!"

With that problem so generously solved, Camilla was still confronted with writing to the Marquis de Fouchet. Throughout the day while she served dutifully in the shop, she ran over and over in her mind what she should say. At last the solution seemed clear: in case the old gentleman proved to be long dead, the missive must be short— simply giving the bare facts stated in the deed of entitlement; her name, address, age, and the fact that she knew not where to seek for friends or relatives of her noble family. She ended: "I pray you help my cause if 'tis possible, my lord. Your faithful servant Camilla de Courville."

She sat for a long time staring at that signature—how easily it had come from her pen; yet how unfamiliar it still remained. She had hesitated to put "Countess" as well, and instinctively felt this was correct; certainly her grandmother had not given her title at the closing of her long letter. When the envelope was sealed, Camilla held it close to her breast for a moment, praying: "Oh, dear God, Father of us all, may the Marquis be still there to receive it."

The following morning, she shyly slipped into the pharmacy and handed it to Mister Castle who, seeing the earnestness in her face, swore that it should go out on the very next mail packet.

So now there was nothing left but to wait. She refused to even consider that the waiting might prove in vain. Now that the tide of her fortune was beginning to turn—to bring her dreams of taking her rightful place in the *haute monde* to fruition—there must be no doubts, no fears. Had the Marquis already died surely *someone* in his family would read her letter?

As always her refuge lay in thinking of Sir Michael. His particular elegance, his kindness, the warmth of his rare smile had lit a lantern in her heart which could never be extinguished. She kept her resolve never to linger on the corner of Curzon Street for, that way, he might recognize her dressed as a shop girl. No, her next meeting with him must be as a perfectly gowned and coiffed member of the elite—a young woman far removed from The Crown Tavern—but oh, how she ached to catch even one glimpse of him!

Days passed into a week and Camilla's hopes rose then fell when no letter came from France. She asked Mister

Castle how long it took for such missives to reach France and he explained, "The Packet service is much improved these days—I find that replies reach me from Grasse within six or seven days. I declare you are anxious to hear from your friend but you must have patience, my dear. You say he is aged so I warrant he may be sick or has, perchance, moved to the country."

In spite of his advice for patience, Camilla found her thoughts a trifle morbid and despairing that day. She imagined her letter lying, ignored, on the floor of a grand house long deserted because the Marquis was dead.

So hard were such ideas to throw off that she scarce noticed a group of three customers entering the shop, for Mistress Castle was seated behind the counter where she served the afternoon purchasers—the duchesses and such —for two hours each day. Camilla went on with her task of placing new phials of perfume on a shelf.

Then a deep, familiar voice stayed her hand and she stood rooted to the spot, her back to the company. It was Sir Michael and he sounded irritated:

"Now pray, Augusta, do not shilly-shally all day over making a simple choice! Why you demanded that I accompany you I cannot imagine since I have promised to pay for any birthday gift you wish for."

"Oh, Michael, do not bully me so! I declare we are no longer children and, knowing your penchant for charming objects, I thought you might find this pretty shop intriguing. Mama and I find it so, do we not?" The voice was young and far from assured; Camilla found her breath coming more easily—for a moment she had feared the worst, that Sir Michael was accompanying his wife, but only an elder brother would dare to address a girl so. She half turned her head to look at them, praying with all her soul that he might not recognize her.

They were a striking family, mainly because of the vast difference between the elderly Lady Monford who possessed the height, grace, and handsome looks which she had passed to her son, and the daughter called Augusta

70

who, at seventeen, was plain, dumpy and of a placid good humor. Her only claim to beauty lay in her eyes, more amber than brown and flecked with gold edged by silky long lashes. Camilla warmed to her—perhaps because she was Sir Michael's sister and not his wife; but she did not bother to analyze this unworthy emotion.

Mistress Castle had risen and bobbed a small curtsey to Lady Monford, obviously a valued customer during her rare visits to London, and they entered into pleasant conversation over Mister Castle's latest creations.

While Augusta roamed somewhat helplessly along the shelves, Sir Michael stood pointedly not far from the door. Without being told to do so, Camilla went to the girl's assistance and Augusta smiled gratefully.

"Pray advise me for I declare mama has never thought me old enough to warrant such perfumes before. Yet, soon I am to make my debut—once I have taken the correct lessons in dancing and deportment, of course, for I confess I move like a horse cart at present, or so my cruel brother informs me!" She darted a teasing glance in his direction which made him look around with an affectionate, if impatient, glance. Then his eyes strayed to the beautiful girl just behind her and, for a moment, his gaze grew penetrating while Camilla quailed inwardly. Then he turned back to scrutinizing the paved street beyond the window.

The likeness was remarkable, true, but it was impossible that a common harlot from an East End tavern could be assisting a prim woman such as Mistress Castle in a fashionable shop patronized by all members of society. Yet the similarity was certainly there and stirred uncomfortable memories.

For, in spite of his outright disgust when he left The Crown on that fateful night, the face he had loftily dubbed "charming" had continued to haunt him now and then. That girl was depraved and wicked no doubt, but such beauty was never to be found in the high circles in which he moved and, subconsciously, he searched for it among

71

the young daughters of the nobility. His young sister had spoken truly when she said that he loved beauty and sought it eagerly in old books and the paintings of great masters. It fulfilled some inner need of his nature by which he knew he could never wholly give his heart unless the woman of his choice satisfied this need in addition to possessing a lively mind and strong character as well.

With a surge of relief that he had wondered, then dismissed the thought, Camilla renewed her attentiveness to Augusta wishing only to please her. Phial after precious phial was opened, sniffed, and then hesitated over—as were the beautiful boxes of soap; yet Camilla did not harrass the girl. It was enough to sense with every fibre of her being that her true love was here, close to her, albeit he was impatient to be gone.

At last Lady Monford addressed her daughter: "Come, Augusta, surely you have made your choice by now? We are to take tea with the Duchess of Wentworth and you cannot waste Mistress Castle's time much longer!"

Poor Augusta blushed crimson and appealed to Camilla:

"Pray—you choose for me! They are all so perfect I know not whether to choose this—or this—or that delicious one over there! And as for the soaps . . . ."

Sir Michael turned and abruptly addressed Camilla for he most ardently wished to be gone—gone from the sight of the shopgirl who curiously disturbed him:

"Wrap the lot," he ordered sharply. "Perfumes, soaps—whatever has caught my sister's fancy. No price will be too high." He almost added the words "to escape" but bit them off in time. Escape from what? A thorn in his memory which had set his taste in women to an apparently unattainable height? Oh, he would ride after this—ride hard around Rotten Row since it was too late to go further afield, and dismiss all such ridiculous fancies from his logical mind.

With fingers that trembled a little, Camilla did as he bid. Collecting three of the most expensive perfumes and two

72

boxes of soaps, Camilla tied an immaculate parcel and left Mistress Castle to name the price—she knew that her voice was unusually low and melodious and did not want Sir Michael to give her such a penetrating look again.

Yet, as they went from the shop, Camilla, with an urgent hunger in her heart, managed to be close to the window so that she might watch the Monford family walking up Cavendish Row until they were out of sight. *As a countess,* she reflected, *Lady Monford would accept me gladly, and Augusta could so easily become my friend*—the friend she had never had in her life and whom she could trust. And, as they turned the corner out of view, Sir Michael carried her heart with him, more ardently dedicated than ever.

Her longing, nay craving, to hear from France increased a thousand-fold. London's grand season was scarce a month away, and Camilla most passionately longed to take her rightful place in the festivities. Yet, without word from the Marquis, her search for the de Courville relatives stood at a dead end.

On the following morning, when Camilla was in sole charge, Miss Augusta Monford came to the shop unescorted. The younger girl seemed a trifle nervous and unsure of herself but Camilla's heart warmed to her again:

"Why, Miss Monford, this is a pleasant surprise, I declare. How may I help you?"

"I don't know that you can—well, not really"—Augusta twisted her kid gloves in chubby hands—"I—found you very beautiful yesterday. Indeed mama remarked on it, too, though my brother huffed off to his beloved horses!" Her amber eyes held a spark of humor now. "It's easy for him, I warrant, being so handsome and sought after. But—forgive me, pray—I felt you might help me to become more comely." Her eyes roved over the well-stocked shelves. "Some—some face lotions, perchance? Or—or something?"

Camilla came around from behind the counter so that they might talk quietly:

"Alas, we sell nonesuch here, only soaps and perfumes

73

for ladies, but I will gladly help you if I can, Miss Monford. Come, take this chair for you seem a little short of breath."

Augusta subsided gratefully, admitting with a grin, "I fear I seldom take exercise, Miss Castle. Indeed, dancing tries me sorely! I am also presently having deportment lessons with Madame Suzanne and am finding it *very* difficult."

Camilla's gray eyes were so filled with sympathy and understanding that her words gave no offence:

"I fear that there are no lotions or potions in any shop to solve your problems. But, forgive me if I seem forward —perhaps the answer lies in yourself!" She looked the girl over candidly. "You have four or more weeks before your debut, I fancy—ample time to take a little more exercise each day and forego the rich pastries that possibly tempt you?"

"They do indeed," wailed Augusta. "Surely they do no harm—have nothing to do with being comely?"

"They do indeed, I assure you Miss Monford!" Camilla laughed. "You have the most beautiful eyes—and pretty hair, I declare; nothing prevents you from becoming a beauty save a little too much weight. Oh, 'tis presumptuous to speak so, I beg forgiveness but—you did ask my help and I have no other to offer!" *What would Mistress Castle say should she come in now?* Camilla wondered. Her advice was quite uncalled for in such frank terms to the daughter of a wealthy, valued customer.

"I fear I have seemed rude," she added with contrition.

Augusta rose, smiling. "I warrant you most certainly have not, Miss Castle. You have spoken nought but the truth and, though 'twill be hard to forego the pastries and sweetmeats I so enjoy, I will do my best, I swear."

"And you will succeed, Miss Monford," Camilla assured her with a glowing smile.

After Augusta Monford had gone, she pondered long over the unexpected conversation and a small flicker of fear brushed her heart: drawn by liking and sympathy,

74

she had talked at length to Sir Michael's sister—talked, indeed, as her natural self and not the reserved "Miss Castle" of the shop. But what if her most earnest prayers were answered and, by some miracle, she, too, was enabled to make her debut as Countess de Courville this very season? She would meet Augusta on equal terms at every turn and there was no hope, now, that the girl would not recognize her as the friendly adviser at Maison Castle. It would seem a fine jest, no doubt, and Augusta would tell not only her mother and her new acquaintances but Sir Michael, her brother. How gossip would fly!

Plunged in gloom, Camilla felt that her longed-for future in society was suddenly doomed. Worse, far worse, Sir Michael was bound to confirm his vague suspicion that the shopgirl, the newly presented countess, and the girl whom he had so sadly misjudged at The Crown were one and the same . . . .

Camilla closed her eyes, fighting desperately against both gloom and hopelessness that were so alien to her spirited young nature. If only, if *only* word might come from the Marquis . . . .

When two weeks and two days had passed since Mister Castle took her letter to be mailed, Camilla was resigned to the fact that there would be no reply, ever. Yet, surely there must be other people in England who could assist her? Her parents had come seeking them so they had to exist. But where could she find some clue—some hint of where to search?

Vainly she read and reread the brief, tragic little missive from her mother, pored over her deed of entitlement, then flicked, despairingly, through the long letter from the Countess Claudette—if only she could understand one word of her native French!

The thought crossed her mind that Mister Castle must know the language and would be glad to translate it for her. But she soon dismissed the idea: if Fate had raised her hopes only to dash them to the ground, then she must remain as she was, a humble shopgirl earning her keep and her title would have no meaning.

That night she slept little, tossing and turning as one impractical plan after another whirled through her mind: might the prince himself be convinced by the deed? Yet the endless talk she had overheard of his extravagance and greed for money put this idea firmly in its place—only if she could approach him laden with wealth and jewels would he even lend an ear to her plea. Each plan as it occurred to her was dismissed: lawyers, duchesses, even a small notice in *The Court Sheet* appealing for any friend of the de Courvilles to come forward seemed impossible and foolhardy.

Mistress Castle was in a waspish mood next morning, chivvying Camilla into extra tasks that were not hers by right. Yet she did not argue for she was too weary in mind and body.

It was with relief that she escaped into the shop as nine o'clock struck and set the door wide to the morning sunlight. Mistress Castle had declared her intention of remaining in her sanctum to rest the pain in her knees, so at least in the shop there would be peace.

Catching sight of herself in a mirror behind one of the shelves, Camilla was astonished that no signs of her inner tension appeared on her face, the gray eyes shone clear as ever and her skin glowed softly. This strange fact that no outward signs remained of the tortured night, fascinated her. She was still gazing at her reflection when a light step and a tactful little cough behind her startled her and she swung around.

No customers came at such an early hour but there, inside the door stood an elderly man of small stature, watching her as he leaned on a gold-topped ebony cane. His white hair powdered in the old-fashioned way was brushed carefully over a hair-pad to give it a grander sweep away from his forehead. He was clad in black save for a snowy cravat and ruffled shirt front with white lace ruffles at his wrists. There was something birdlike in his alert blue eyes as he continued to stare at Camilla with lively interest which gave no offence.

"Ah!" he spoke at last in a silvery, high voice. "I need ask no further for 'Camilla de Courville'; come close to the light, child, for I declare my eyesight is no longer as it were." Although his English was perfect there were slight foreign overtones here and there, especially in the way he rolled his r's.

Mesmerized, and hardly capable of hope, much less coherent thought in her astonishment, Camilla moved toward him.

He waited until she was scarce a yard distant, then raised a beautiful quizzing glass set in gold filigree and held it to his right eye, examining every detail of her lovely face in complete silence. At last, with a sigh, he dropped the glass back on its chain and held out a frail hand to her.

"My dear girl, you are the living image of your grandmother, my immortal Claudette!" His blue eyes grew moist with memories. "Never, never had I thought to behold that exquisite visage again in this sad world!"

Camilla woke from her trance and her whole being flooded with affection and thankfulness.

"My lord—you are the Marquis de Fouchet! Oh, how I have prayed God that you would come, that you might be still living and receive my letter . . . oh . . ." She, too, was overcome with emotion as the full meaning of this man's presence struck her with wonderment.

"You spurn my hand, Camilla," he said with a touch of reproof. "Yet that will prove I am, indeed, very much alive!"

Blushing with shame, Camilla seized it and, on impulse, raised it to her lips and kissed it. "I had no hope but you," she spoke urgently. "Yet I never intended that you should travel from France in answer to my poor letter!"

"I did no such thing," said the Marquis. "No, the good God was with us both for I have lived in London these many years with my wife and 'tis only once a year that I venture across that unpleasant sea to visit our Chateau near Paris. 'Twas pillaged, naturally, by those damn rebels, but it stands—oh yes, it stands and a faithful couple keep it in fair order. I happened to be there when your letter came and, forgive me, I did not hasten my return on your account. I fear I considered it the work of some imposter. Yet now—now that I behold the young Claudette standing before me, what can I say?"

"Marquis, I will fetch you her letter—'twas to my late mother, I believe and—and I am shamed to admit I know no French!"

"A letter from Claudette—and you cannot read it! Oh, child, I am come in the nick of time I can see—pray fetch it quickly and also that deed you mentioned to me for everything from now on must be done *trés comme il faut.*"

Without a thought for Mistress Castle or her wrath if she found the shop untended and a French aristocrat waiting there, Camilla sped up the twisting stairs on wings. In less than a minute she returned, bearing her treasure with her which she thrust into the Marquis' hand.

" 'Tis all there, my lord—even the sad note my mother penned just before my birth."

She stood quietly, curbing her surging impatience as to what would happen next, while the Marquis let his eyes dwell, lovingly, on the yellowed paper and fading ink of the long letter penned by his early love. Then he looked up.

"With your permission, dear child, I should like to borrow these precious pages to read quietly at leisure, for they evoke so many memories, I declare, so many."

"Most certainly, my lord, " cried Camilla eagerly. "And, if I may visit you one day would you translate a little of it for me?"

He nodded absently, for he was studying the lawyer's deed with great attention. At last he looked up.

"What, precisely, is your position now, Camilla?"

Her beautiful eyes met his with absolute candor.

"I work here for Mistress Castle, earning my keep by doing things to help her in the house and then serving in this shop. I—I fear I have no fortune, as the few words written by my mother will explain. Perchance you will help me to find some relatives? De Courvilles who came to England after the revolution—who might tell me of our lost estates and where I might turn for help in recovering them?"

"Help? Relatives?" The small man sounded quite peppery and Camilla drew back, abashed. What had she said to offend him? He quickly went on, however: "This is no time to relate your family history, child, but unless I am mistaken, you are now the only surviving de Courville. Your exquisite grandmother had but one son, your father, and from him had come but one child. As to the estates, I fear you would find small comfort or fortune in those sad ruins. No, from now on you must forget all care and entrust your future to me—and to my so charming wife, naturally."

"You?" Camilla gasped. "Oh, sire, I never dreamed—I did not expect . . . I did not intend to presume."

"Presume, tcha"—he dismissed it with a twinkling eye—"I must confess to having a great deal of money and no heirs. To fulfill your grandmother's wishes I would do vastly more than take on one extremely lovely girl. Now—where is this Mistress Castle? I would have words with her immediately."

"I—I will fetch her, my lord." Camilla still felt stunned as she moved toward the door leading to the sitting room.

"No, no, I wish to speak with her privately. Unless she be still abed, pray take me to her."

Trembling, Camilla tapped on the door—Mistress Castle would be mighty put-about at this intrusion, but the Marquis was close on her heels and he said with a hint of impish mischief, "Do not shake so, Camilla—you have no need to fear dragons any longer!" And, without waiting to be announced he went into Mistress Castle's private domain and closed the door behind him.

79

Camilla, her knees threatening to collapse under her after the astounding developments of the past half hour, leaned against the shop counter and began, to her horror, to laugh! Weak it certainly was and closer to mild hysteria than mirth, but it all seemed so preposterous—even the little Marquis himself. However, at least Mistress Castle had not stormed out in one of her fits of temper.

The small silver clock chimed ten—from now on early customers might arrive and, at the very thought, Camilla mustered her wits and pulled herself together. All she could hear from the sanctum was a continuous murmuring of muted voices.

Two or three young blades strolled in and she prepared to serve them in her usual, reserved way, forestalling their flirtatious quips which she had long learnt to value at their true worth—nothing. Yet, as she wrapped packages, received payment, heard herself exchanging polite "good mornings," her mind was once again in a whirl, but no longer of despair, only of great joy and excitement. What, precisely, did the Marquis mean when he declared that he would "take on one extremely lovely girl?" Was he offering her a home outright, or merely promising to place her somewhere suitable? Oh, if only he or Mistress Castle would emerge from their conversation and state clearly what the future held! It seemed nigh on a lifetime since the old Marquis had closed that door; yet a glance at the clock told her it was but scarce twenty minutes ago.

As the clock chimed the half hour, the door opened and, led by the Marquis, Mistress and Mister Castle followed, both looking more than somewhat bemused. But Mister Castle strode forward, raised her hand and, bowing over it, kissed it.

"Countess, may I congratulate you on coming into your own? No wonder you were so impatient to hear from France!" His eyes were smiling and Camilla smiled back.

"I know you are very forgiving, Mister Castle, I—I fear I lied a little about the Marquis being an old friend! Only I declare he was a dear friend to my grandmother!"

Mistress Castle subsided into her chair behind the counter, quite overcome as she dabbed her eyes.

"To think—a titled young lady has been set to cleaning out the fires! Oh, the shame of it—'twill be all over London, I swear."

Camilla went to her quickly. "No, Mistress Castle— pray have no such fears on my account. In fact the jest would harm me more greatly than you, I vow. May we make a pact between us now on this happy morning: let us swear faithfully to keep my service here a secret—I beg you to pledge it as I do with all my heart."

"Oh, my lady, you are so good, so kind," murmured Mistress Castle weeping with gratitude. The Marquis was growing restless.

"It's all arranged. I shall now tell the Marquise de Fouchet so that all will be prepared for you on your arrival at our house on the morrow. My carriage will await you at four o'clock sharp in Berkeley Square."

They all stared at him as he walked briskly away, then Mistress Castle's innate snobbery emerged in sheer wonderment:

"Just fancy, my lady—you are to reside in a grand mansion a scant hundred yards from the residence of His Royal Highness!"

Camilla could take in no more for the moment. Instead she put a protective arm around Mistress Castle's shoulders and held out a slender hand to her husband who grasped it gratefully:

"Pray, pray let me remain simply 'Camilla' to you both, now and always. You have shown me such kindness and let me come into your home when I had nowhere to go. It's a debt I can never repay but 'twill live in my heart."

And deep in her very soul Camilla sang: *"Tomorrow!"*

Chapter Six

Mistress Castle had insisted on presenting Camilla with one of the blue print dresses she wore in the shop and, although very simple, it looked fresh and charming beneath her creamy pelisse and straw bonnet. She was very nervous, as on the stroke of four o'clock, a splendid liveried footman presented himself at the shop door saying he had come to accompany the Countess de Courville to the carriage.

Her farewells to the Castles were brief for she had sworn to visit them very soon with all her news. Now, holding her small head high, she followed the footman to Berkeley Square where he opened a door of the de Fouchet carriage with a flourish. Camilla was hard pressed not to gasp out her delight, for it was by far the handsomest equipage she had ever seen: shining black with gilded ornaments and a magnificent coat of arms painted on each door. She stepped quite regally inside, feeling every inch a princess as she sat on the tasselled, velvet upholstery.

But she sat very upright, straining for a first glimpse of her new home and was not disappointed; the mansions in Carlton Terrace were stately, white, and splendid beyond belief. As the carriage drew up she steeled herself for the meeting to come. But she need have had no fears for a butler led her across the marbled hall to the salon, all in white and gold, where the Marquis awaited her in front of a vast fireplace while the Marquise, a tiny figure of great elegance, sat in an armchair. Both were smiling a welcome as Camilla, overcome, swept her very finest curtsey. The Marquis spoke:

"Very pretty, child, but there is no need for such formality." He turned to his wife: "My dear, allow me to present the Countess Camilla de Courville—Camilla, the Marquise de Fouchet."

The Marquise held out a tiny, birdlike hand bejewelled with valuable rings which Camilla dutifully kissed.

"Pray stand straight, my dear." The Marquise had a voice of firm authority behind the tones of a silver flute. For a time her brilliant dark eyes studied the slender form in front of her, noting with approval the large, shining gray eyes, the glowing, magnolia skin, and fine bones of the small face, and then dwelt on the sweep of red gold hair under the cheap bonnet. At last she nodded and smiled warmly:

"Camilla, you have great potential. Did my husband inform you that your grandmother was *la grande belle* at the Court of King Louis?" And without waiting for an answer, she continued crisply: "But, *mon Dieu,* we have much, much to do if you are to make your debut. Gowns, many, many fine gowns and a coiffure that shall be *perfection.*"

A true French aristocrat to the tips of her small, black satin, diamond-buckled shoes, she gesticulated expressively with her small hands as she talked: "Those clothes you wear are deplorable." She pronounced the word in the French manner and the "r" rolled out most disapprovingly. "I refuse to be seen driving to my dressmaker with a Countess disguised as a mere servant wench! De Fouchet!" Her husband sprang to amused attention and Camilla, surprised, soon learned that the Marquise always addressed her husband thus. "Send the carriage immediately to bring my dressmaker, Monsieur Paul, and also my coiffeuse this very evening." She turned back to Camilla: "I shall have you transformed, *Cherie,* in what the English refer to as 'the twinkling of an eye'—so crude! No, it shall be done more swiftly in the French manner—by good management!"

Touched as well as amused, Camilla felt instant affection for the grand old lady while her gratitude went also to the Marquis for he was about to spend a fortune on her transformation. She knew that this emotion had been a true, living thing, possibly the most important experience in his life. Yet it puzzled her a little, for the deep affection between the old man and his wife was almost tangible in its strength. In truth, with age and his growing disillusionment over his own beloved France, the Marquis had enshrined his youthful love for the famous beauty as a symbol of all that was lost and gone. Since it was never requited, it stood perfect, without any regret, as the grand romance that had been such a feature of life at the French court in its hey-day.

The Marquise understood and cherished her husband's long-lost dream. It was a refuge from the enforced exile to England. For she, herself, had no complaints. Love, deep and lasting, had grown between her and de Fouchet when he was more mature—long after Claudette had removed herself to her husband's Chateau on the Loire. Indeed, his early, unattainable love had but made their own the stronger since, in the early days, he told of his youthful peccadillo with rueful self-abasement. Only recently had he resurrected his dream, as old men do.

Watching their faces, Camilla loved them both—indeed it was the only repayment she could make for the tide of miracles they had caused to surround her life.

The afternoon coffee, which was wheeled in on a rosewood trolley, Camilla had never tasted in her life, since it was a French habit; but the delicate cup that was handed to her frothed with cream, seemed to her like pure nectar.

Soon, the mansion became a hive of eager industry; Monsieur Paul, a tall, sophisticated man of French origin was the most expensive designer of gowns in London.

While she stood in her chemise and petticoats in the splendid bedroom allotted to her in the de Fouchet mansion, Camilla alternated between delight and fear as the Marquise and Monsieur Paul conversed in eloquent French, interspersed by many gestures of delight, despair, and even fury as measurements were taken, patterns of rich materials spread out by his minions and designs sketched in midair. Then, suddenly, she understood that the two elderly people were old friends, delighting in indulging their native passion for argument—a passion neither understood nor shared by the English. Contented, Camilla submitted, allowing them to treat her as a doll— a dummy figure—but one of whom they approved as worthy of such attentions.

Shortly after Monsieur Paul left, the coiffeuse arrived— a vastly different character being small, fussy, and afflicted by a tic under one eye which gave him the appearance of continually winking. However, once he had brushed out Camilla's glorious hair and surveyed her from every angle the wink was forgotten.

"A la pauvre Princess Charlotte," he declared, standing back as the Marquise nodded complete agreement. Although Camilla was only to learn this fact later, the princess had been the adored child of the Prince Regent who died shortly after making a brilliant marriage.

Camilla closed her eyes against the firm clip-clip of shining scissors. Mama had always affirmed that her long hair was a glory—to be tended and polished like a jewel. Now she closed her eyes as the heavy curls fell away and still the busy scissors snipped.

"Ah, c'est bien—trés bien, Monsieur Guillaume."

Camilla wanted to cry out, to lift her hands up to protect her head—but no, that would be folly. After all, had she not prayed to be transformed into a grand young lady? And suddenly another thought came to cheer her: once her hair was so altered and she was dressed in the most exquisite gowns, surely not even Augusta Monford would recognize her, much less her brother? A small pulse of excitement began to beat in her temples—she longed to open her eyes and look in the mirror; yet knew she must wait until the Marquise expressed final approval.

When the scissors ceased at last, she felt the expert French hands of Monsieur Guillaume combing and lightly flicking tendrils into place on her forehead, before smoothly combing up longer strands at the back into some arrangement on top of her head and deftly securing them. It was complete.

At last the Marquise clapped her hands in delight: "See, pray see, Camilla! I swear you will fancy meet a stranger!"

Slowly Camilla opened her eyes wide—and stared. It could not be herself—this girl with a perfectly shaped, small head supported on a long, slender column of white throat. Her hair just as shining as before but now framed her small face in delicate ringlets with a small bunch of curls held by a golden ribbon on the crown. Slowly, nervously, she smiled at this reflection while the two older people waited, beaming. At last, in a slightly shaky voice, she said:

"I declare, you have made me *pretty!* Oh, 'Tis a miracle!" for she had never given much thought to her looks before.

"Pretty?" scoffed the Marquise. "Pfui! You are *beautiful,* my child—the most beautiful girl in London, and must comport yourself as such."

Humbly, Camilla thanked Monsieur Guillaume who, all smiles announced:

"You will attend my salon each morning, Countess, so that I may make *les petits* arrangements to suit your engagements."

Dinner was served at nine o'clock by candlelight in the vast dining room which, on occasion, had seated a hundred guests.

"Gasoliers make this place lonely when we are dining à trois, but candles! Romantic and friendly, I feel."

Indeed it was, the soft light flickering on gleaming silver and priceless crystal. Only Camilla found herself unwarrantably sleepy. It had been such a day of change, far beyond her girlish dreams. Suddenly a pang of guilt startled her to wakefulness. The Marquise was saying:

"Alas, tomorrow will prove quiet, Cherie; even Monsieur Paul cannot wave a wand and produce charming toilettes until the day after, and I declare, you must never again be seen in that common blue dress."

"Then, I wonder . . ." Camilla began hesitantly to ask yet another favor, "might I, perchance, visit Mama? Dear, kind Mrs. Fernaby who tended my poor mother and then brought me up with such care? I desire to tell her of your kindness and of my change of fortune? Oh, I will go quietly from your kitchen entrance, I swear," she added quickly, "for Mama lives in the East End of London, in Cheapside, and 'tis scarce three miles on foot."

The Marquis and his wife exchanged glances—their lovely protégée possessed a warm, loyal heart—a rare quality, these days, among the *ton*. The Marquis spoke eagerly:

"You shall certainly not proceed on foot, Camilla—no, you shall have a carriage and bring back this 'Mama' for we must thank her, must we not my dear?"

The Marquise raised her eyebrows, then smiled a little. Her de Fouchet was so impetuous! But yes, they owed this woman gratitude at least. Then she added to Camilla:

"You must sit well back during the drive, however— for I will *not* have you exposed to public view looking so *bourgeois!*"

Camilla was radiant. "I swear, Marquise—indeed, 'twould alarm poor mama if I were to appear much changed. I will cover my head with my bonnet also, until we return here, for she took much trouble with my long hair."

And so it was arranged. Camilla chose her time care-

87

fully—mid-afternoon when, if fortune favored her, Thomas Fernaby would be gone to some cockfight or bear-baiting and would not see the grand carriage.

But in this, fortune failed her: the landlord of The Crown was in a choleric ill-humor: that leader of the raffish set among the rich young bucks, Sir Caspar Randal, had taken to pestering him nightly to produce "The Peach" as he dubbed his blurred vision of Camilla— indeed, if she were not forthcoming soon, Thomas feared that his valuable new clients would take themselves elsewhere and his bordello revert to a common bawdy house.

When Camilla entered quietly through the back door, he was haranguing his cowering wife:

"You have hidden that milk-sop girl, Hannah, and I demand you fetch her back or 'twill go sorely with you. I'll—I'll break every bone in your . . ."

"No, Mr. Fernaby, you will do no such thing," interrupted Camilla evenly, her courage rising to defy this petty tyrant. "At last I am free to tell you of my hatred— my scorn for your mean ways and cruel treatment of Mama!" She turned to a bewildered Hannah while Thomas stood agape, his drunken wits scattered to the winds.

"Fetch your bonnet and shawl, dearest Mama, for I have come to take you on a visit." Unconsciously, her new environment and the secret knowledge of the fashionable coiffure hidden beneath her simple bonnet had given Camilla a new air of authority—the tone of an aristocrat addressing a minion. "Furthermore, Thomas Fernaby, if you dare from now on to lay one finger on your wife I shall remove her to safety!"

Mrs. Fernaby was equally astounded but hastened to do Camilla's bidding. As the girl escorted her tenderly to the carriage, Fernaby lumbered through to the tavern where he watched with cunning, bloodshot eyes as the splendid carriage drove away: so the wench was putting on airs, eh? Had found herself some wealthy protector and coveniently forgot all the past debts she owed her everloving father? Well . . . he would see.

Meantime, clasping mama's still trembling hands in hers, Camilla poured out the story of her good fortune as the carriage bore them swiftly away from Cheapside. Soon Mrs. Fernaby forgot her husband, his threats, and all the hardship of her life as her heart swelled with great joy and thankfulness: beloved little Camilla had, so rightfully, come into her own at last.

With Camilla's hand reassuringly still gripping hers, Mrs. Fernaby did her best to overcome her awe at the great house as she was led in to the grand salon to meet the Marquis and his wife. They behaved most charmingly, knowing exactly how to put her at her ease.

Camilla had removed her bonnet in the carriage, fearing tears from mama but instead: "Oh, Camilla, it becomes you to perfection, I declare," exclaimed Mrs. Fernaby. "Why, I'd scarce have known you 'tis so elegant! And you are to have gowns to match. I vow, you'll set all London on its ears as, indeed, you deserve!"

Sitting on the edge of a gold brocade settee beside the Marquise, Hannah Fernaby tasted coffee for the very first time and expressed her pleasure. From then on, although the interview was brief, it held warmth. The Marquise summed it up at the end by saying:

"Mrs. Fernaby—I swear you have done well—nay, royally by the de Courville family—it must have cost you dear and we are indeed grateful. Camilla speaks beautifully, and she can read and write with fluency—a pleasing attribute, since many parents in society set more store by needlework and playing horrifically on the pianoforte."

The visit was a success and, although the Marquis insisted that his carriage convey Mrs. Fernaby back to her home, she halted it some distance from The Crown saying it would be more politic to arrive quietly.

For the first time Camilla felt emboldened to kiss the lined, parchment cheeks of her two benefactors and they were touched:

"Pray forgive such liberty," she begged, a trifle fearful. "But mama means so much to me."

"Quite right, my dear," said the Marquise gently. "Without her loving care I doubt you would be the young woman you are now."

On the following morning the first of Monsieur Paul's toilettes arrived. Overawed on her first day in the de Fouchet household, Camilla had not dared to ask the Marquise any questions as to color, fashions, or anything else about such magnificent gifts. Yet she was enchanted —the colors proved the very ones she might have chosen herself; cream, pale gold, subtle gray edging toward silver, green, white, and chestnut. And, the Marquise informed her, these were a mere beginning—grand ball gowns were still to come.

"But, meantime, there is much work to be done, my child. You hold yourself well, I declare, now you must learn to move with graciousness at all times—to carry your head with a small air as befits your rank. You shall attend deportment classes with Madame Suzanne." The Marquise gave her a small chuckle. *"La pauvre,* she is in truth a Mrs. Brown but, it seems, French names are all the thing in London and her teaching is excellent."

Madame Suzanne! Camilla thought worriedly to herself. Surely that was the name Augusta Monford had mentioned that day she had come alone to the shop to seek Camilla's help in improving her looks. Her delight at her new world hesitated for a moment—at these classes her first real test would come. Would Miss Monford recognize the shop girl who had befriended her beneath the elegant trappings of a countess?

Then her spirit rose proudly to the challenge—the road ahead was beset with possible mischances, but was it so discreditable to have earned her living before the de Fouchets came to her aid?

"You shall also have dancing lessons," the Marquise continued, outlining her plans for Camilla.

"Dancing!" Camilla's eyes glowed but she made a rueful moue. " 'Tis very difficult, I warrant!"

"Nonsense!" The Marquise sprang up from her chair like a young girl and, raising her hooped skirts a trifle, for she still favored gowns set on small hoops at the sides giving full skirts which suited her, she pointed a delicate satin toe and proceeded to execute a charming minuet.

"Voilà! No doubt that is a bit old-fashioned, but I declare 'twas my favorite in France. And remember, *Cherie,* all those handsome young men that will partner you, sadly they have little skill on the whole. All that horse riding and such blinds Englishmen to the more delicate arts, I fear."

Camilla laughed, her fears partly banished. She thought of Sir Michael, and felt sure he would cut a dash at a ball.

Aloud, she said, "I will work hard and do my best to please you, Marquise—indeed, to dance beautifully, floating around some grand ballroom has long been a cherished dream."

"Now you will succeed, I warrant. Only you must not think of pleasing *me.*" The steel discipline was back in the light voice: "You will do well in order to honor the proud title you bear, my dear—to follow worthily in the footsteps of your grandmother."

The Marquis had entered and heard this remark: "I vow she was the most beautiful dancer I ever saw in my life!" A touch of longing still lingered in his old eyes.

When Camilla had left them, the Marquise tapped him lightly on the arm with her fan: " 'Tis shame the *Belle Claudette* never loved you, my poor old de Fouchet." Yet her tone was amusedly sympathetic. "You are a dreaming fool, my dear—but a pleasant one."

He patted her small hand and retorted gallantly, "You forget that I had not yet met you, my Michelle, and a man's first great love is always enshrined as a goal beyond reach."

On the following morning Camilla surveyed herself carefully in the tall cheval mirror that had been placed in her bedroom. Her gaze was not for self-admiration, but a clear appraisal of the change in her. It was, indeed, complete—but was it sufficient? The charming morning toilette of russet, ribbed silk in the Empire style certainly outlined her slim figure as no common dress had ever done. After Monsieur Guillaume's morning arrangement of her coiffeur, the shining curls and tendrils of dark gold showed to best advantage under a small velvet hat perched at a daring angle with two fine osprey feathers curling down on to her neck. Since the morning was warm the only addition needed was the long, soft kid gloves that reached to her elbows and a pretty gilt mesh reticule suspended from her wrist on a gold chain.

She smiled. "I believe Augusta will be hard put to it to declare me 'Miss Castle.' " She spoke the words aloud to give herself extra assurance.

Madame Suzanne's classes in deportment for young Ladies were held in a large, bare room in Dover Street, Mayfair, that was hired in the evenings for musical recitals and dramatic monologues. Apart from a shrouded pianoforte and music stands, the only furniture was up-turned chairs lining the walls and piles of heavy tomes brought by Madame herself.

Fifteen young ladies assembled that morning, among them Camilla and Augusta Monford. The girl was certainly less plump, Camilla noticed with pleasure, and Augusta's glance only rested on the young countess with admiration and not recognition. They were all commanded to remove both hats and gloves. Then Madame Suzanne placed a heavy volume squarely on the crown of each head and, beating time on the floor with her cane, commanded:

"Walk! Heads well up, form a circle, turn right and place each foot steadily in front of the other: one, two, three and four and five—Miss Tremayne, Lady Daphne, your books are slipping—now six, seven—Miss Monford do not shuffle, I pray—step out . . . ."

After walking endlessly in a circle the books were not removed. Instead, Madame commanded:

"Now, holding your heads well up, you will curtsey; first, two steps to the left and down—then two steps to the right and repeat!" As they struggled to obey, some letting the books fall to the floor, Madame moved among them using her cane to tap a reprimand. "That is good, Countess—splendid. But that *will not do,* Miss Monford! I declare you scarce bent your knees at all—perform by yourself and let me see a graceful movement!"

Poor Augusta cast an appealing glance at Camilla who had seemed to sweep down and up all in one movement. Knowing Augusta's deep timidity, Camilla asked:

"May I do it with her, Madame? Perhaps I can help Miss Monford."

From then on Augusta clung to her throughout all the exercises and, when the class ended, she said:

"Oh, Countess, how can I thank you? I vow I shall never hold myself well and mama will be ashamed of me!"

"Of course that will not happen," Camilla encouraged warmly. "If you fancy it would help I will ask the Marquise de Fouchet, with whom I am staying at Carlton Terrace for the season, if you may be invited to take coffee with us. Then we can practise the exercises before the next class."

Augusta clutched her hand in an ecstasy of gratitude. Their friendship had begun. And Camilla's hardest bridge had been crossed.

Camilla's first dancing class followed on the same afternoon. Mr. Mainwaring scorned to take a French pseudonym to increase his standing. He was, quite simply, the finest exponent of dancing in England and preferred to teach each pupil separately in their own homes. This

93

gave them half an hour of his undivided attention and, when required, his expert partnership. His charge was exorbitant, but every mother of an aspiring debutante, paid gladly for the privilege.

With him he brought an accompanist—for if a grand house possessed no pianoforte it was not worthy of his attention. But at the de Fouchet mansion he expressed himself very satisfied. The Marquise possessed a music room in which she held soirées and, when the servants had cleared the furniture back against the walls, there was an expanse of parquet flooring which Mr. Mainwaring declared: "Perfect, Madame La Marquise, I declare quite perfect."

Camilla was nervous. Deportment came easily to her for she had long ago learned to hold her head high in Cheapside as a child. But dancing—that magic portal to success, filled her with alarm.

But, after one thorough look at the young Countess, Mr. Mainwaring fell under her unconscious spell: here, to benefit from his guidance, was the undoubted beauty of the season. With many girls he despaired, but this one— this priceless one—was to be his success. He commenced his lesson in a different way. Leading Camilla to a chair he called to his accompanist:

"Play—play each fashionable dance so that this young lady may be acquainted with the rhythms." Surprised, the small man obeyed.

Gradually Camilla found her feet tapping—her eagerness to move to the seductive valses, polkas, and galliardes mounting. Without warning, Mr. Mainwaring swung her out on to the floor and, side-by-side they circled around until she was following his steps with ease. Then he turned to face her, placing a light hand on her waist and then the real dancing began.

"Oh," she cried at the end, "it's a glorious sensation, I declare!"

"Your partners will be fortunate indeed, Countess. I shall work you even harder on our next lesson."

So the days progressed and, imperceptibly, Camilla felt her confidence growing. She *was* the Countess de Courville and the fear of being challenged receded. More importantly she was making friends with the other young ladies in the deportment class, but especially Augusta Monford whose admiration was unfeigned. One morning, shyly, she said:

"Mama says I may invite you to take tea with us, Lady Camilla. Will you come?"

For one breathless second Camilla felt that the world was spinning away beneath her feet—she was invited into Sir Michael's house in Curzon Street! Never again would she stand on the corner, a waif adoring him from afar, for now—even though he almost certainly would not be present—she would see the interior, see the furnishings and treasures among which he had chosen to live and be able to envisage him there.

"It would be delightful, I declare," she said warmly. "You are very kind, Miss Monford."

"Oh, *pray* call me Augusta," cried the other. "I so want us to be friends and Miss Monford sounds so formal!"

"Very well—if you, in return, will simply call me Camilla; a title seems a trifle absurd when one is so young." And she laughed—laughed secretly at herself, also, for to possess a title had been the pinnacle of her young dreams and here she was, in a position to call it absurd!

Augusta blushed with pleasure: "If you will not think me presuming," she began, then added with a rush, "indeed, I *think* of you as Camilla to myself for it's such a pretty name." Collecting herself, she added eagerly, "I will beg mama to send a footman with a formal invitation this very day!"

When Camilla told the Marquise of this pending invitation, the Frenchwoman beamed and patted her shoulder. "It is good, *Cherie,* very good that you make friends already. But this afternoon, directly after your dancing class, I wish you to don that enchanting afternoon creation by Monsieur Paul—the cream silk—for I have a most par-

95

ticular friend of my own that you shall meet. I pray you make a fine impression for she can assist your season more than I can."

"Oh, dearest Marquise, who can it be?" asked Camilla, impressed.

" 'Tis Mrs. Fitzherbert."

"Mrs. Fitzherbert! Surely—is she not . . ." All the ill-natured gossip that she had overheard at Maison Castle flooded into Camilla's memory and she was at a loss for words.

In a pique, the Marquise flicked open the small fan that was always suspended from her wrist on a black silken cord and used it with short, impatient movements to show her annoyance:

"Kindly remember, Camilla, you are still a mere child and in this house I will hear no gossip or other things of ill-nature when you speak of a dear friend of mine! Mrs. Fitzherbert is a true wife and dear companion of His Royal Highness and 'twill be great honor indeed if she becomes your champion! Why, you might receive a personal command to attend the first Royal Ball of the season at Carlton House!"

"I—I meant no harm, Marquise," gabbled Camilla, filled with contrition and, anxious at all costs, not to offend. The Marquise smiled and closed the fan.

"Very well, *Cherie*—you will come to the salon at four o'clock precisely, and behave with perfection. You are a charming girl and I wish my friend to see you at your best."

"You are most kind, Marquise." Camilla felt it wise not to risk any further contretemps by asking the hundred and one questions that crowded her mind about this most distingushed visitor.

When her dancing class ended, she sped to her bedroom, having but a scant half hour in which to prepare herself for this important meeting. However, the Marquise had instructed her personal French maid to attend the young countess on this occasion. So Camilla found her exquisite cream silk already laid out with its matching slippers and Marie ready to assist and then, with deft touches, adjust her coiffure. At five minutes to four the maid said:

"Is time, Countess—time you descend."

Camilla felt unduly nervous—this was the first big test the Marquise wished her to face and, with her inbred awe of royalty it seemed most alarming. As the hall clock chimed four, she opened the door of the salon, stepped inside, and swept her very best curtsey before advancing to be introduced.

Mrs. Fitzherbert was anything but the *femme fatale* gossip had somehow painted her, instead, Camilla saw a cheerful, buxom figure upholstered in dark blue faille, a hat larger than fashion favored, perched with many jewelled hatpins on her mass of graying curls and at least two chins. But her jewels! They alone were enough to proclaim her unofficial status as court favorite. Camilla found it difficult not to stare, for the diamond and ruby necklace surrounding the plump neck gave off flashes of fire with the heavy, massive rings on her plump hands rivalling it closely.

The Marquise presented Camilla who, again, made a smaller curtsey before saying in her melodious voice:

"I am indeed honored, Madam." For "Madam" or "Ma'am" was the accepted address for a royal princess and Mrs. Fitzherbert was completely won over. She patted the settee beside her and Camilla sat down, upright yet meek while she was scrutinized through a jewelled quizzing glass. From then on nothing more was required of her for, having bestowed her unstinted approval of the young Countess de Courville, Mrs. Fitzherbert proceeded to discuss her with the Marquise as though Camilla were a deaf mute.

Incredulously, she heard her finer points discussed—plans for a most dazzling debut into society outlined and, when she had finished the cup of china tea served to her by the Marquise (for the prince insisted on everything

97

from furniture, objets d'art, and tea to be Oriental), Mrs. Fitzherbert patted Camilla's knee:

"Prinny will love you, my dear," she chuckled in her rich, claret-oiled voice. "He never tires of a pretty face and you are *extremely* pretty, child; oh, yes, you will be the Toast of London—and Brighton, for I insist you must visit us there."

On which accolade she rose and made her farewells, leaving Camilla dazed as all the golden gates seemed to swing open ahead of her—now no longer dreams, but reality.

Chapter Seven

During the three days prior to her taking tea in Curzon Street with Lady Monford and Augusta, Camilla was quite bewildered by the number of invitations delivered by liveried footmen praying the honor of the company of the Marquis and Marquise de Fouchet and the Countess de Courville.

But the Marquise was most satisfied. "It's splendid, *Cherie,*" she exclaimed. "Cotillions will improve your dancing, while at soirées you will meet all young members of the *ton*. True, the music is dull, but what would you? I fear de Fouchet will not accompany us for he detests such affairs, but 'tis no matter."

It made Camilla anxious that the Marquis appeared little except at luncheon and dinner, and she feared that her coming might have upset the even tenor of his elderly life —and she owed him so much. One afternoon she tapped timidly on his library door as he rose from a deep leather chair to welcome her with much pleasure. He poohpoohed both her gratitude and her apologies for creating some disturbance in his house:

"My dear child, your coming has brought nothing but delight! I declare you have brought such joy to my beloved wife that I have no longer the bad conscience! No, for many years I have preferred to live quietly among my books for I am too old to enjoy the endless chatter of society, yet I could not entirely desert the Marquise on every occasion so, for her sake, I endured it."

Camilla noticed that her grandmother's letter lay open on a small table close to his hand—treasured relic of his dead love. And she knew, then, that she must not intrude on these memories by asking him to translate it to her; besides she would know nothing of the people and the times of France so long ago. Yet, she was glad she had visited him and need feel guilty no longer.

She was extremely nervous as the carriage bore her to Curzon Street to take tea. *Would* Sir Michael be there? Perchance he might be putting himself out a little to help his young sister during her debut. Yet, just to be arriving at his door in style was miracle enough. Ascending the three wide steps, she glanced along to the corner where she had stood so often watching for a glimpse of him. Then the door opened and a butler led her through a wide hall, whose walls were hung with riding and hunting trophies. He then ushered her into a charming petit salon, obviously furnished for Lady Monford's personal use. She and Augusta were alone and their welcome was smiling:

"I am enchanted to meet you, Countess de Courville, for I declare Augusta chatters of you from morning 'til night! You have helped her greatly, I understand, and I am grateful."

"She has become a dear friend, Lady Monford," Camilla assured her. "I delight in her company."

"Tho' I swear you are not the very first to help me, Camilla," Augusta laughed. "No 'twas a pretty girl serving in Maison Castle." She looked at her friend more intently. "Imagine! She bore some slight resemblance to you, I declare—but of course she could not compare with your beauty and chic!" she added quickly.

Oh, pray to the dear Lord above that Sir Michael thinks the same! thought Camilla inwardly. Then the two girls were eagerly scanning the invitations Augusta had received, placed proudly along the mantlepiece, and discovered that many were the same as Camilla's.

"I shall enjoy every one," stated Augusta firmly. "Although the cotillions alarm me, I confess. But Mama has made my brother promise to escort me now and then," she giggled happily. " 'Twill be support, I declare, but lud! How he taunts me if I don't excel and I'm still a poor dancer, I fear!"

"Nonsense," cut in Lady Monford. "During your last dancing lesson you performed charmingly—Mr. Mainwaring said so."

"Oh, him," scoffed her daughter. "He's so old! It's handsome young beaux that will make me feel awkward."

"The Marquise tells me that few of them can dance," Camilla laughed gaily. "We have only to bedazzle them with our eyes and splendid ball gowns while they trample on our toes!"

Tea was brought in and, as she poured, Lady Monford said:

"At least that is not true of Michael, my son. I took pains to see that he had some social graces by the time he reached eighteen. I must introduce you to him, Countess, at Lady Carlington's cotillion—her parties are always delightful."

The visit was a complete success and Lady Monford thoroughly approved of her daughter's new friend.

On her return to Carlton Terrace, Camilla found Mrs. Fitzherbert deep in conversation with the Marquise; as soon as Camilla appeared she held out her plump hand in greeting, beckoning her to sit at her side:

"We have been plotting on your behalf." She gave her deep-throated chuckle. "For I insist on playing a large part in your debut! So we have been drawing up a list of the most suitable young gentlemen for your attention, my dear. I shall see to it, personally, that you are introduced to them all; soirées make me yawn, but cotillions I enjoy and, since Prinny is still absent, Taking the Waters in Bath —which I detest—I have few evening engagements. Now," she went on briskly, "the young Duke of Walsford is the most eligible since he is both wealthy and also owns magnificent Walsford Place in Surrey. Charming profile, too, even though perchance he is a trifle dull—but you will soon correct that, I swear. Then comes—"

Dazed, Camilla heard name after name, coupled with their fortunes, titles and prospects. But there was no mention of Sir Michael. Tentatively she interrupted.

"I have just taken tea with Lady Monford who promises to present me to her son, Sir Michael. Is he not included?"

Mrs. Fitzherbert burst out laughing: "Michael Monford? My dear, he has a heart of stone! I declare he has reached the age of twenty-eight and never once lost his head, even to the most charming of girls. Mothers despair of him, even tho' their daughters have been known to go into a positive decline for love of him. No, I doubt even your beauty, Countess, will storm *that* bastion!"

Camilla's own heart thrilled to this news—her Sir Michael—her deep, secret love, had never philandered as other young men did. Yet surely, when they met, she could pierce his indifference by the very strength of her own feelings?

Meantime, twelve exquisite ball gowns had been delivered by Monsieur Paul and also more demure evening toilettes for soirées. Camilla spent the whole of one blissful afternoon displaying each in turn for the approval of the Marquise. At the end, the elderly Frenchwoman declared:

"Oh, but he is *splendid,* my dear Monsieur Paul! I shall inform him of my pleasure. Now"—she thought for a moment—"yes! The white and gold, embroidered with our proud emblem of the Fleur de Lys must be set aside for the Royal Ball."

"But—surely we have received no invitation?"

The Marquise waved her small hands. "My child, such an invitation is a royal command! It is issued a scant day or two before the date yet all members of the *ton* cancel their engagements in order to attend. Oh, 'tis inconvenient at times, of course, but to refuse would be unpardonable."

And so Camilla braced herself for her first two public

presentations in society, since both were musical soirées. They were, as the Marquise had warned, a trifle tedious, but Augusta and Lady Monford were present and the two young girls—in particular the beautiful French countess, attracted much attention in the intervals when refreshments and champagne were served. On the first occasion Camilla met the Duke of Walsford and, in spite of his splendid Roman profile, dismissed him from her list since his opening gambit was:

"Er—Countess—are you, by chance, interested in Hogs?"

Camilla opened her gray eyes wide in inquiry.

"Pigs, y'know—I fancy breedin' 'em at Walsford and, by jove, they're fascinatin' animals, I declare. I shall be charmed if you will visit the new styes I'm buildin' close to the home farm."

Politely, Camilla explained that her social diary did not allow sufficient time. Instantly his interest in her waned and she felt free to move on into another group.

If only it were a cotillion and Sir Michael was present!

That came four evenings later. Camilla and Augusta had taken to visiting each other's homes without formality since both families approved of the connection, and Augusta was filled with excitement:

"I am to wear a blue ball gown to Lady Carlington's cotillion and 'tis bewitching. What color will your gown be—for we must not clash!"

"The Marquise insists on deciding for me—but 'twill not be blue, I swear, since I have none in that shade."

"You are so beautiful already, Camilla, but pray, pray look your very best, for my brother is to be there," she hesitated, a little shy, as she added: "You are such a dear friend and oh! I would fain that you were a sister, also! There, that is mighty forward—and yet I swear you will find Michael a fine man indeed! I know he is but a baronet and, no doubt, you will marry a prince so my hope must seem foolish."

"Not at all." Camilla's color had risen: "I care naught

103

for rank but vow I will marry only the man of my choice!"

If only dear Augusta knew that her brother was, indeed, already the one to whom her heart was pledged. But she must never forget Mrs. Fitzherbert's warning that Sir Michael could not be swayed by a pretty face.

That afternoon she waited anxiously while the Marquise chose first this gown—then another; all were perfect but Camilla had certain preferences and, at last, the choice fell on her own favorite—a pale gold that complemented her glowing hair and shining eyes; with it came a necklace of gold and finely matched amber as well as satin slippers with amber rosettes.

The Marquise appeared queenly in pale violet velvet with a diamond necklace and three ropes of matched pearls. In the carriage as they drove toward Lady Carlington's house she said:

"You are trembling, *Cherie!* Nervousness is unwarranted for you can now dance well and have you not acquired two beaux after only two soirées? Tonight will bring many more, I swear."

Only one mattered. Receiving floral tributes from Lord Datchet and Sir Edward Simmonds had been pleasant, of course; yet now Camilla scarce remembered their faces since they had not made a deep impression on her with their flowery, affected conversation.

To her delight Mrs. Fitzherbert stood close to Lady Carlington as the guests arrived—and the setting for her first true meeting with Sir Michael was as ideal as Camilla could have wished. The regency house designed by Nash himself, who was so transforming Brighton, had high ceilings, tall, gracious windows. The lovely decor in cream and gold seemed almost hidden by great banks of camellias, hothouse carnations, and roses interspersed by feathery greenery. In the Grand Salon, where dancing would take place, a four-piece orchestra was already playing some airs from Mozart to welcome the guests, and Lady Carlington's personal welcome was warmth itself.

As Camilla was presented by the Marquise, Mrs. Fitzherbert whispered something into her ladyship's ear:

"*Now* you see the Beauty of the Season!"

Lady Carlington held out both hands in greeting. "Marquise, how charming of you to bring the Countess de Courville—I see her reputation is not misplaced." Then, to Camilla: "You are indeed welcome, Countess, for I declare you will add much to my simple evening!"

They passed on into the Grand Salon where several guests were already assembled. Camilla eagerly scanned the faces to discover the Monford family but they had not yet arrived. Instead, she grew aware of an intense scrutiny and looked up—then her heart jolted most uncomfortably: staring at her in puzzlement was a tall, fair young man with one eyebrow raised as he struggled to place her.

It was Sir Caspar Randal, whose drunken, lecherous face was as indelibly printed on her memory as Sir Michael's handsome one. For some reason she had never expected to meet him on respectable, social occasions, deeming him to be a frequenter of taverns and brothels now blessedly out of her life. Yet here he was. Feverishly, she began to think of ways to avoid dancing with him—the memory of his hot, greedy hands gripping her so wantonly, could never be forgotten.

Fortunately, the Marquise was at her side, guiding the evening as she interrupted:

"Pray do not fill up your dance card just yet, Camilla —there are many guests to come."

Although she kept her back resolutely turned toward Sir Caspar, he strolled across within a few moments and addressed the Marquise in an affected drawl:

"The Marquise de Fouchet? Allow me to present my-self—Sir Caspar Randal, at your service. I wonder whether I may have the honor to ask your daughter for the pleasure of a dance later on?"

The Marquise found him not unpresentable, but she detested his assumed affectation, and so she replied:

"Indeed, Sir Caspar, I fear this is not my daughter but my Ward—The Countess de Courville—but I have bade her not to fill her card at present as we have many friends arriving."

It was a polite snub and Camilla managed a small, frosty smile which half-convinced him that she was not, indeed, really like the tavern wench at close quarters and he had no choice but to move away.

Camilla breathed more freely—then her heart beat very fast for, among a crowd of newcomers, she could clearly hear the voice of Augusta. *He* was here!

Mrs. Fitzherbert was shepherding several people toward her, including the Monfords, and Camilla, while welcoming Augusta and her mother with delight, did her very best not to stare at the splendid figure cut by Sir Michael in evening dress—after all, he was supposed to be a stranger. She allowed Mrs. Fitzherbert to make the introduction herself, a trace of mockery in her voice to remind Camilla that this was the unattainable young man—the one with a heart of stone!

Camilla raised her wide, shining eyes to his as he bowed over her hand then straightened to his full height and smiled down at her. Then his glance lingered, a trifle baffled, and her heart beat even faster: was he remembering after all? The moment before he bridged the pause seemed like a lifetime, but his voice, when he addressed her, was deep and warm as she remembered:

"I am enchanted, Countess and, for once, my little sister has not exaggerated the beauty of her friend!" Camilla blushed and felt shamed that she could not lower her eyes as modesty decreed—to have him close, paying her such a charming compliment, even if it were mere good manners, was the stuff of her dreams. Besides, he looked so handsome in his royal blue velvet coat, the edge of the high collar and the breast stitched elegantly with silver above his white breeches and silver-buckled shoes.

"You are most kind, Sir Michael," she replied graciously, "for, as with Augusta, this is my first cotillion and like Augusta, I confess I am a trifle nervous." Her face lit with an enchanting smile. "Our dancing master is most civil but to dance in public is something of an ordeal I find."

"Then pray allow me to claim the second dance." He lifted the card suspended from her wrist by a golden silk cord and scanned its emptiness. "I cannot believe the young men have been so hesitant!"

"Oh, 'twas the Marquise who forbade me to accept any requests until most guests had arrived," Camilla assured him swiftly. "Now I fancy they have."

"Then let me be audacious and ask for one more—the sixth? Then you shall tell me how you are faring. I am booked to take Augusta onto the floor for the first valse since she has more cause to be nervous than you, I swear." His signature against the numbers was clear and firm and Camilla tried to appear quite calm—for one dance with him she had prayed, but *two!*

"You are trusting, Sir Michael, I warrant"—her eyes twinkled, teasing him—"but I swear to release you from the second if I prove too inept!" With tremendous effort she turned aside to permit the presentation of many other young men who now felt able to beg a dance from this beautiful stranger in their midst.

Sir Caspar missed none of it and, after a few minutes, advanced to make his request again for indeed the young Countess *did* resemble the tavern doxy he desired so passionately. Fortunately, by then, Camilla was able to exhibit a full card and say with seeming honest regret:

"Alas, Sir, I fear that I have been besieged—on another occasion, perhaps?" At which point her first partner came to lead her out.

Inwardly, Sir Caspar fumed; petty to his very core he took any rebuff of his wishes much to heart and Camilla had made a dangerous enemy. Happily quite unaware of this fact, she found, to her delight, that her dancing now came naturally and her nerves vanished. By the time Sir Michael encircled her waist lightly with a long, slender hand, she had no fears of venturing into the lively polka and he proved Lady Monford's words—he was a superb dancer. It was a dance that permitted little conversation but their laughing eyes met frequently and, at the end, he said:

"I declare your dancing talents equal your beauty, Countess!"

She was in a daze of delight and excitement until he claimed her again—this time for the more intimate valse. He asked about her French origins:

"I trust, being French as I understand, you will not find English society too different from your own, for I declare you will greatly enliven our season."

"I fear that I can make no comparison, Sir Michael, since I have never lived in my native country. The revolution stripped the de Courvilles of all their estates and possessions and I have been brought up here, in quiet seclusion, until the Marquis and Marquise de Fouchet adopted me as their Ward—they are old friends of my family."

His next words dashed her growing hope that he found her more to his taste than other young ladies: "Well, I can see you have already made conquests this evening—without doubt we shall be dancing at your wedding before many months have passed!"

After that, Camilla managed to study his behavior with other partners when the conversation with her own proved boring and their steps clumsy. It brought no comfort, for with each one, his smile was warm and his attentions assiduous. Sir Michael was simply socially accomplished and, try as she might, she could read no more into his seeming warmth to her.

In the carriage on their way home the Marquise was exultant: "Oh, *Cherie,* you are to be congratulated! I declare you have more than fulfilled my hopes since, already, two young peers as well as most desirable young gentlemen have craved the right to pay you their respects!" She gave her silvery laugh. "I swear that our afternoon coffee will be invaded by your would-be suitors after tonight!"

It was a hollow triumph and Camilla, after dutifully expressing her gratitude, went to her room and wept after a seeming success.

On the following morning, Augusta Monford called eagerly on her friend, filled with elation:

"Camilla—what did you think of my brother? Pray, is he not the handsomest man in London? I declare he asked much about you when we returned home! He swears you remind him of a painting."

Or a humble girl in a tavern, thought Camilla sadly for her spirits were still low. Had she not danced, twice, in the arms of the man she loved and yet made no more impression upon him than other pretty girls?

Undaunted, Augusta hurried on to relate her own small successes: "Sir Christopher Stanwell *and* Mr. Edwards, who is mighty pleasant, have asked permission to call! But, will you believe it, Michael has sworn to attend more functions with me than ever before? Tell me, I beg, did you not favor him just a little?"

"He is handsome indeed, just as you promised," Camilla assured her friend truthfully, then added wistfully: "But I believe Mrs. Fitzherbert to be right—he is never swayed by young ladies of fashion. Perhaps he is too occupied with his studies—and horses."

Augusta laughed happily: "Nonsense! He demands perfection in all things, Camilla, and he already admits your beauty! Mama was mighty intrigued when he said so last night."

On this slight crumb of hope Camilla began to recover her natural gaiety. And if he had agreed to accompany his sister more often during the season then she must surely meet him frequently. To be more worthy of his company, Camilla ventured to approach the Marquis de Fouchet in his library—might she study some of his heavy tomes on art—on music, and some volumes of poetry?

The old man was delighted. "My dear child, pray share my own passions in life when you have time. My dear wife tells me that you are already a success and much sought after—but knowledge is never fickle."

And so, in quietness, Camilla often sought his storehouse and found it enormously rewarding: when she again met Sir Michael her conversation might not be so trivial, for art in particular delighted her, filling her senses with new vision.

For a whole week he did not appear, either at soirées or cotillions, but Augusta explained that he was in the country breaking in a young stallion. Meantime, the Marquise was proved right since charming young gentlemen presented themselves at Carlton Terrace each afternoon at five o'clock. Not one of them inspired emotional response in Camilla, but their lively conversation taught her much about social interchange and helped her to feel more at ease.

Then Sir Michael returned to London and, although he kept his promise to escort Augusta to functions, he scarce appeared eager to seek out Camilla more than once during an evening.

However, Augusta had her own dream between her teeth—to win Camilla as a sister as well as a dear friend, and she reported her own observances:

"I think, Camilla, that my brother is afeared of you!" she giggled.

"What nonsense you talk, Augusta," laughed her friend. "I swear I am certainly not alarming and Sir Michael is no coward!"

Augusta looked mysterious. "No, no—I mean afeared that he might fall in love with you. You are claimed for every dance but I am not and so I have watched him— oh, such long, dark looks he bestows on you while you are circling the floor, you have no idea!"

A small thrill went through Camilla. "But surely, such looks are meant to convey dislike?" she asked.

"Whoever heard of langourous glances conveying dislike? I declare, the truth is you do not care for *him!*"

Camilla had proved that Augusta was a friend to be trusted and suddenly her longing to pour out a little of her true feelings was overwhelming:

"Oh, Augusta, indeed I *do!* In truth, he scares *me* by his seeming avoidance of me at present. I—I fell in love with him when—when I saw him out riding one day." That, at least, was almost true for, even to Augusta, she dared not confide her vigils on the corner of Curzon Street. "I confess, lately I have been studying much in the Marquis' library so that I might converse the better with Sir Michael—only he gives me no chance."

Augusta's delightful amber eyes were alight with excitement: "Indeed, you truly love him, I can see! Come, we must devise plans, seek ways in which you two may talk quietly. Perhaps at his house one afternoon?"

Camilla was horrified. "I will have no part of such a plot," she declared roundly. "Why, if you are correct in thinking that he is afraid of loving me, what could be worse than forcing my company on him? Oh no, Augusta—you mean well, I'm sure, and I know little about men at present, but instinct tells me they must never be chased after."

Augusta's face fell. "I did not think," she agreed humbly. " 'Twould, indeed, do no good since Michael has been shamelessly pursued by girls for many years and considers them ninnies. Yet I so wish to further your love, Camilla."

"Then keep my secret locked in your heart and let things take their natural course, my dear." Camilla smiled, deeply touched by such concern. "A propitious time will come, I know it."

And it did, indeed, on the following evening. Both families were invited to a soirée by the Duchess of Wentworth, close friend of Lady Monford and Sir Michael's godmother, so he could scarcely refuse; besides, the

111

Duchess had good taste and had hired a much sought after quintet of musicians to entertain her guests.

Perhaps Augusta did connive a little, but it was not apparent as the Monfords took their seats and Camilla and the Marquise chanced to be placed next to them. More than that, Camilla found herself sitting beside Sir Michael who acknowledged Camilla with a charming smile. The program was devoted to the works of Mozart whom she had recently studied in a biography written shortly after his untimely death, and she decided to seize her chance.

By his warm applause she guessed that Mozart was a favorite composer in the eyes of the man she loved and, turning to him, her gray eyes glowing, she said:

"What exquisite music he wrote—I have always been saddened that he died so young, and in chronic poverty as well! With his genius what magnificent symphonies he would have given to us in addition to the ones we have already. Why, we might have rejoiced in fifty such instead of only three!"

This time Sir Michael's expression was not only surprised but admiring, and he turned toward her eagerly: Camilla de Courville possessed culture as well as ineffable beauty which he had feared to test in case it merely covered a vapid mind.

"I see that we share at least one great interest, Countess. Have you heard much of Mozart's work?"

"Not near enough," she smiled wistfully. "It's not considered *comme il faut* for young ladies to study serious matters, but I would like to hear his operas which I am told are very fine."

"You shall," he promised with ardor: "I have travelled to Germany to hear *Le Nozze di Figaro* and am determined that it shall be performed here, in London—I mean to place the question before the Prince himself for, if he leads the way then perhaps society might cease to be so prudish! 'Tis true the theme is a trifle risqué but what matter when the music is magnificent?"

When the musicians returned, Camilla's heart was afire with fresh hope—her studies, though a trifle rudimentary in such a short time, had not been in vain and she prayed that a chance might soon arise to discuss painting with him since the Marquis' volumes were packed with glorious illustrations and, of all subjects, it was her favorite.

Some inner reserve in Sir Michael seemed to have melted away and he gave the beautiful young countess his full attention during the rest of the evening, bringing her refreshments and champagne during the longer interval as they talked of the older masters, Bach and Beethoven, with Sir Michael unwittingly providing much information to sustain Camilla's own comments.

At the next cotillion, Sir Michael claimed not one but *three* dances, and Camilla deftly turned the conversation to art for they were in a grand mansion famous for its old masters hanging on every wall.

Sir Michael scarce dared to believe his good fortune—was it possible that he had discovered his ultimate dream? Perfect beauty allied to an intelligent mind?

He had quite forgot Camilla's slight resemblance to the tavern wench when he chanced to encounter Sir Caspar Randal at White's Club. Sir Michael would have evaded him but Sir Caspar made this impossible, his public rejection by the young countess arousing all his petty spite.

"Ah, Monford, it seems our latest beauty favors you! But has it not struck you how closely she resembles the choicest harlot at The Crown?" He chuckled, "I swear they might be twin sisters except that *our* famous beauty is prim and imperious which bores me to distraction." His eyes sharpened. "I do not pursue her since I can enjoy, nightly, the beguiling charms of her 'double.' Why not sample them for yourself?" he sneered.

Sir Michael found the whole matter distasteful: "I do not frequent brothels," he announced with cold scorn, moving away. He promptly dismissed the unpleasant meeting from his mind.

But, watching him go, Sir Caspar's face twisted with

hate and jealousy—a jealousy he had always felt for the handsome looks, great charm, and huge wealth of Monford. Now he had Camilla to add to all these—Camilla who fired Randal's blood as no woman had ever done until possessing her had grown to a fixation in his warped mind. Have her he *must* for the very thought of Monford, of all men on earth, being free to kiss that lovely mouth, embrace her slender body at will could not be borne. There were ways to foil his rival—there had to be, and Sir Caspar made up his mind.

That very evening he would go to The Crown, catch Thomas Fernaby late in his cups and offer that mean soul gold for the information he sought: that the "Countess," as he scornfully dubbed her in his mind, and the doxy girl once at the bordello, were one and the same he did not doubt for a moment. Could not doubt for, by proving it, he would hold the lethal weapon to destroy them both publicly. At least if he, Randal, could not have her Sir Michael never should.

And were not the girl's origins uncertain? His hopes rose.

Chapter Eight

Glorious buds of hope were opening in Camilla's heart and a new radiance possessed her. For now, at each function, Sir Michael sought her out as eager to talk as to dance with her. His wary guard had vanished forever and, as he waxed eloquent on one of his favorite subjects his tone was almost boyish. Camilla caught his enthusiasm and, every morning, she spent hours in the Marquis' library, anxious to increase her own knowledge. Indeed, she could truly say that her interests almost matched Sir Michael's own.

The growing relationship did not pass unnoticed and famous hostesses smiled and nodded approval. A few lovesick girls sighed and swore they would go into a decline but youth is very resilient and, when even they could not remain blind to Sir Michael's absorption in the lovely Countess, their hearts obligingly turned elsewhere for the season abounded in handsome young beaux.

Sir Caspar was quite content to watch from the sidelines, his smile more a quiet smirk of secret satisfaction for, at last, he held the power to bring the great romantic dream crashing to the ground.

Things had worked out very well for him. He had waited until he remained the only customer at The Crown, then slapped down four gold coins in front of the Scottish landlord:

"Mind you, they'll have to be earned, Fernaby," the young man said firmly. "I'll add another one if you give me the information I seek. I wish to know the whole truth about the new young beauty come lately into society—the *Countess* Camilla de Courville. And stap me, if she isn't the living image of your pretty doxy who refused my advances—ain't that strange, Fernaby? Pull yourself together, man—I want the truth!"

Thomas Fernaby focused with some difficulty on the dazzling guineas before him for his eyes began to fuse with hatred as well as drink.

"Countess, eh?" he spat onto the floor. "Well, I'll tell ye about this fine lady, sir, and gladly." He took the precaution of covering the money with his large hand. Then, words falling over themselves, the whole story came tumbling out, laced with years of bitterness and loathing for the girl's cussedness against her poor old "father"—her cruel ingratitude.

Sir Caspar drank it all in, taking care not to interrupt the flow. At last Fernaby cursed Camilla with every foul word at his command, ending, "Jest you bring yer fine 'Countess' back here, sir—I'll beat the life out of 'er."

"Oh, I don't think that will be necessary," said Randal calmly, placing the extra guinea on the counter—for he had, indeed, had value for his money. "I can think of a far more harmful punishment—and, oh yes, she'll suffer, make no mistake on *that* score."

Camilla was completely unaware of the threat Sir Caspar Randal was posing to her happiness. In fact, she hardly ever noticed his occasional presence in the background at the various functions she attended.

Augusta declared herself delighted beyond all words. "Oh, Camilla, Michael will speak ere long, you'll see!" she laughed merrily. "I declare he is grown quite absentminded at home, scarce hearing a word that Mama or I address to him. He is much changed, I swear!"

And Camilla smiled gently. "There is no haste, Augusta —why, the season is scarce begun!"

116

Yet it was about to do so in great style. Mrs. Fitzherbert came to call one afternoon, her kindly face alive with pleasure and excitement.

"My dear, dear Marquise, his Royal Highness is returned to London! Is it not splendid news? I declare I am as happy as a young girl newly in love, and there is far more. See, I have brought the invitation to you myself," and, from her muff she drew out a most impressive envelope heavily embossed with the Royal Arms in gold. Inside was a thick, gilt-edged card, far larger than any ordinary invitation and also bearing the Royal Arms. Camilla gazed in awe.

It was for the Royal Grand Ball and, beneath the names of The Marquis and Marquise was her own: The Countess de Courville.

Impetuously, Camilla bent and kissed Mrs. Fitzherbert's plump cheek, her eyes alight with excitement.

"Dear, dear Mrs. Fitzherbert, including my name was your kind doing, I know it! Oh, 'twill be the greatest occasion of my whole life—in fact I swear, I feel nervous already!"

Mrs. Fitzherbert beamed as did the Marquise:

"Nonsense, my dear, I declare I shall be Hostess and you will find my Prinny most benign for I mean to present you to him myself. He will eye you through his quizzing glass which many girls find a mite daunting, but 'tis only that he may see you more clearly. I have already told him that you will be the belle of the ball and be a fine asset to the entire season!"

Camilla blushed at such compliments and stammered her further thanks. To crown the day, Augusta came to call a little later bubbling with the news that all the Monfords had also been invited.

"And you will look so beautiful and receive such royal favor, I declare, Michael will be quite carried away!"

Camilla looked at her with true admiration.

"What a wonderful friend you are, Augusta—I truly believe you have not one jealous bone in your body! But you, too, are becoming a beauty, you know, and I refuse to let our relationship be one-sided. Tell me, which beau do you favor most so far? You have helped me so much I would fain help you now if I can."

Augusta looked down demurely, although her smile was roguish.

"Truth to tell I have half lost my heart to Mr. Edwards; of course mama expects me to wed a Duke at least; yet none could be as congenial to my taste as Brent Edwards —he is a most amusing and sympathetic companion. Also, unlike Michael, he does not require great brains in a wife, which is fortunate," she giggled happily. "Oh, how studying bores me to death! But Mr. Edwards has a splendid house in Chelsea and is very wealthy I fancy, so perhaps mama will come to see him as I do."

"I swear that she will," Camilla agreed warmly. "After all she loves you dearly and surely your happiness will always come first in her consideration?"

"I trust so—and oh, Camilla, I pray that he, too, will be attending the ball for I have a truly magnificent gown. Why, it makes me feel like a princess since it is purest white with silver flowers as a motif, and I declare I even appear *slender!*"

That evening, at a cotillion, the talk was all of the Royal Ball and it seemed that every girl making her debut amongst the *ton* had received an invitation. Sir Michael, as was now accepted, engaged Camilla for three dances and, during the first he teased:

"I warrant you will have far grander partners than I at such affairs, Countess. Indeed, I am tempted not to attend!"

Such was their relationship that Camilla felt safe in retorting:

"Come, you are no *coward,* Sir Michael? Why should I desert a friend for strangers?"

He sighed, serious now. "You hold a high position indeed, you know. I declare a countess ranks scarce an inch beneath a duchess; besides, there will doubtless be many elegant French aristocrats present who are associated with your family and they are much given to charm and flattery, I understand."

Camilla laughed deliciously. "Flattery? By my faith I cannot stand it. 'Twill be pleasant to meet gentlemen who have a connection with the de Courvilles since I know so little having been brought up in England, but I vow my loyalty lies here."

For a moment she thought she had been too forward, too daring in such a statement, but Sir Michael smiled, the trace of anxiety gone from his dark eyes.

"Then I may venture to claim one dance?"

She looked down with renewed modesty: "I shall be grievously hurt if you do not."

Sir Caspar, watching them as always in the background, smiled to himself—his moment of triumph would not long be delayed he felt certain. It gave him an added sense of power that he could gladly allow Monford and the Countess to enjoy this evening unsullied.

On the morning of the Royal Ball, Monsieur Guillaume, the coiffeur, was sorely tried as titled ladies clamored for his attentions. But the young Countess de Courville took priority. He knew as well as anybody that she was already the chosen Toast of London and he spared no pains. Also, her lovely hair was a pleasure to dress and he brought to it all his talent, arranging the short, shining curls and tendrils to perfection and, in completion, tying her small knot of curls on the crown of her head with rich ribbon specially ordered by the Marquise—gold with the French Fleur de Lys embroidered in white. It was a chic complement to her white gown with gold Fleur de Lys.

Monsieur Paul himself condescended to approve the final effect that evening and Camilla was touched, yet amused, at his extravagant flattery, remembering Sir Michael's words. She looked ravishing, however, and only one thing slightly marred the evening: the Marquis pleaded increasing rheumatic pains and had decided to remain in peace at home.

But nothing could dim the sense of occasion as she and the Marquise entered their carriage and drove the two hundred yards to the dazzling entrance of Carlton House. Every window shone from the lights of priceless crystal chandeliers, the awning leading to the grand doors was of royal blue silk edged with gold, and each carriage door was opened by two flunkeys in white wigs, the surcoats of their livery embroidered with the royal arms in rich colors.

And the grandeur of the guests! Some of them Camilla had met already, yet never had she imagined them in such splendid array! Several older ladies had reverted to the white peruke festooned with osprey feathers and gleaming jewels above gowns of rare brocades, velvets, and taffetas over the small hoops favored by the Marquise, while necks and arms were ablaze with diamonds, emeralds, and rubies. The gentlemen equalled this finery, many having coats of cloth of gold, or rich velvets sporting elaborate jewelled embroidery and every shoe carried a jewelled buckle that glinted under the light.

Camilla felt instantly subdued and humble. Her own attire had seemed splendid in the seclusion of her bedroom, yet compared to all this glittering show she felt like a pauper. Having no conceit she could not know that her youthful beauty made her stand out like a rare pearl amid such ostentatious display.

Carlton House, also, reduced her to awe. The Prince Regent had brought his passion for things rich and Oriental to his London house as well as to the Royal Pavilion in Brighton. Above the swaying, bewigged heads, Camilla saw with strange pleasure Chinese tapestries covering the walls of the Reception Hall in delicate, muted colors with fragile figures seated in palanquins, saluting the milling crowd below with ineffably long, slender hands, the finely shaped fingers tipped by gilded nails. A tall bronze gasolier, reaching almost to the ceiling, also attracted her attention: a dragon's head appeared fearsome yet, instead of flames, the hundred tongues blossomed into lotus flowers, each shedding a benign light on the guests.

By then she and the Marquise had almost reached the presentation line where His Royal Highness stood, fat beyond his years yet utterly dominating the scene in his turquoise satin coat, the breast glowing with jewelled royal insignia and his diamond encrusted quizzing glass reflecting every light around him. Beside him stood Mrs. Fitzherbert, encased in purple velvet with a massive necklace of large diamonds and dark amethysts.

As the Marquise and Camilla approached, she held out both hands in welcome while the Prince glanced at her indulgently. She said:

"Pray allow me to present my dearest friend, The Marquise de Fouchet and her Ward, the Countess de Courville who is already the belle of the season!"

The Marquise made a low curtsey and Camilla, in something of a daze, did the same—it all seemed so unreal that she, Camilla Fernaby as she had been for so long, was being received by the First Gentleman in England. Mrs. Fitzherbert's warm heart had foreseen the young girl's nervousness and, grasping Camilla's hands encouragingly, spoke to the Prince:

"See, Sire, I have not misled you as to our undoubted new belle—The Countess Camilla de Courville!"

His slightly pouting lips puckered with concentration as he studied the girl through his quizzing glass and, in her nervous state, it seemed to go on for an unconscionable time but, at last, he smiled in complete approval:

"But you are indeed a beauty, Countess; I trust you also have a lively wit?"

With her most bewitching smile Camilla replied, "I warrant that is not for me to say, Sire." At which he positively beamed:

"At least not tongue-tied I see. You'll break quite a

121

few hearts, no doubt—and 'twill do 'em good, liven 'em up!" He gave a rich chuckle. "I command that you visit us in Brighton."

Seeing the favor bestowed on the new countess, she became the focus of all eyes—especially those that had not seen her. Judging the moment to be right, the Marquis steered her on gently by the elbow into the Great Ballroom and Camilla caught her breath. She found the decor too rococo and flamboyant for beauty, but for extravagant magnificence it was unrivalled.

Then, even before she noticed Augusta, she saw Sir Michael and her heart swelled: he outdid all the peacock colors of other young gentlemen in a startling manner. His coat and breeches were of black velvet above white silken hose and black shoes buckled with pure gold. His high coat collar was fringed with gold while the finest gold lace made the cuffs and fringed his frilled shirt beneath a stiff white cravat. With his smooth black hair and dark eyes, he seemed the very symbol of aristocratic good taste. Then Augusta danced, glowing, toward her and they eagerly admired each other's appearance. Yet Camilla was filled with humility—it could not be possible that she might finally win the heart of a man as handsome and cultured as Sir Michael and she scanned the room which now seemed to her to be filling with far prettier, more elaborately dressed girls than herself. Then he was at her side, his smile and his eyes showing approval:

"Now that you have been so honored by the Prince, I scarce dare to claim the dance you promised me, Countess."

Emboldened, she smiled gratefully up into his eyes and held out her dance card: "As you see, Sir Michael, I am depending on you—else I declare I shall remain a wallflower on this splendid occasion."

His eyes held the teasing expression which she so loved as he took her card:

"I warrant you will never be that! No, you have wisely kept the option to be selective—most girls are far too eager to show a filled card, I fear, as an emblem of success. You are wise, my Lady."

He signed his name twice in his bold script and one, she saw with elation, was the much-prized supper dance! The highest compliment that could be paid to a woman.

After that, as though by a signal, Camilla was beseiged by young dandies, for news of the growing friendship between the glorious countess and young Monford had already been bruited about through most of society. Would she be the girl to succeed in winning his heart after so many had failed? Mindful of Sir Michael's words, she did not hand out her card for signatures but kept it in her own possession, swiftly sizing up the applicant and then either accepting or charmingly refusing each request—the refusals made with seeming sincere regret for she would hurt no feelings.

That she had to wait for Sir Michael until the third dance worried her not at all, for her happiness was now such that her feet scarce touched the ground as she whirled joyously around the floor on every occasion. Could Augusta possibly be right? Might her brother reveal his heart on this most auspicious evening?

His Royal Highness and Mrs. Fitzherbert were occupying throng-like chairs on a dais in a shallow alcove filled with roses, watching when Sir Michael first placed his hand around the slender white and gold waist and took Camilla into a polka. He made a wry face, his eyes laughing:

"Fate is quite shameless, I declare! I have seen you dancing close to His Grace in a valse—then with that ass, Dodswell; now when my chance is come we are forced to prance around like marionettes."

Camilla laughed happily as they sped gracefully up the length of the ballroom: "She will perhaps favor us next time—I hope the supper dance will not be so energetic!"

" 'Twill probably be a gallop to give us an appetite!"

But it proved otherwise. Well aware that gentlemen chose the current lady of their choice for this especial partnership, the leader of the orchestra went into a slow, voluptuous valse. At first Sir Michael remained silent then, looking down deep into Camilla's shining gray eyes, he said slowly: "I know not how to express myself now that the chance is come, for, believe me, I have had no previous experience . . . . but beautiful Countess Camilla, my heart can contain itself no longer tho' you may well break it . . ." He paused as if on the brink of grave danger, yet her candid gaze never faltered. At last he managed: "Not only because you are beautiful beyond belief—and tonight you excel all others—but because my feelings for you are deeper by far. I love you, my dear, not only with my emotions but with my very soul—you are the one I would have at my side for all time."

Camilla experienced a curious faintness from sheer wonderment, and leant, for a moment, against his strong, encircling arm. Anxious, he asked:

"Have I offended you by chance? Do I presume too much on what has been only a warm companionship?"

Instantly the faintness vanished and, holding her flower-like face up to his, her eyes proclaiming her answer even before she spoke, Camilla said:

"Sir Michael, I swear you have honored me more than all the women in the world! I am a trifle overcome by the honor you do me, that is all. For I vow that my heart is— and will be forever—in your keeping."

They could say no more in this royal ballroom, but his hand held her waist more closely and, for a moment— noticed by every dowager seated on gilt chairs and particularly by Mrs. Fitzherbert who smiled—Camilla rested her lovely head briefly against his velvet shoulder as they danced on.

One other spectator, however, had missed nothing that passed between them. Sir Caspar Randal, his cruel heart torn between injured pride, lechery and hatred, had witnessed every move and his secret sense of power rose higher in triumph. His moment had come and, although he had imbibed the royal champagne with alacrity, he was

124

not drunk yet. After waiting so long to win his dastardly revenge—particularly on Monford—a few more minutes were as nothing.

As the music ended, Camilla and Sir Michael lingered a trifle longer on the floor than other dancers, loath to break the physical and spiritual communion between them which formed a world of their own. They would have liked to have been alone in a quiet, moonlit garden rather than surrounded by a throng of chattering royal guests, every one prepared to turn their social smiles eagerly to malicious gossip.

But protocol decreed that they must obey the rules on this very special occasion and so, her arm through Sir Michael's, Camilla steeled herself to walk through a sea of curious faces.

Their mutual happiness proclaimed itself as soon as they entered the vast supper room set with a hundred gilt-legged tables and four times as many chairs. Flunkeys of the royal livery moved deftly among the guests offering a choice of cold Scotch salmon in aspic with spiced mayonnaise and salad, rare cold beef, honey-roasted ham from the royal farms elaborately decorated, cold boar's head, smoked trout, lamb's tongues in herb-jelly, and many minor delicacies.

As Sir Michael entered, so distinguished in his black velvet with the undisputed beauty of the evening, the Countess de Courville on his arm, making such a contrast in her dazzling white and gold, a small ripple of hand-clapping broke out spontaneously among the more senti-mental guests who Camilla was too overcome to acknowl-edge. Her head was still in the stars.

There were but few chairs vacant but an excited wave led the radiant couple to a table for four occupied only by Augusta and Mr. Edwards. Augusta had thoughtfully laid her silver lace stole across the remaining two chairs and they were the happiest quartet in the room.

Indeed, it was impossible to judge which girl appeared the most radiant for the affairs of both of them had moved

125

apace during the dancing. While the two gentlemen chose and ordered supper for the little party, Camilla squeezed Augusta's hand under cover of the tablecloth, and in an admiring whisper told her friend:

"You have fulfilled my prophesy, Augusta—I declare you are grown absolutely beautiful this evening."

Augusta flushed with pleasure and replied, "I swear happiness is the secret, don't you? For I declare you are positively *shining* and never have I seen my brother so happy!"

Then conversation became general for, much as he longed to do so on this royal occasion, Sir Michael's social upbringing knew that it would not be *comme il faut*. First, he must ask for Camilla's hand from her guardians and only then could their joyous news be made public.

Supper that night was served on the famous gold dinner service and, over delicious salmon, there was much carefree laughter. Indeed, Sir Michael wondered why he had found Brent Edwards such a dull creature at various functions for, although not witty, he was certainly amusing enough.

As he raised his glass of champagne, Sir Michael turned to Camilla and, with his lean hand unashamedly covering hers on the table, drank a silent toast of honor to her. With a tender smile Camilla responded in like manner when she took her first sip.

Then suddenly a thin, high drawl, unusually loud and clear, from a table nearby stilled all the gay chatter in stunned horror:

" 'Tis amazing I declare! With great effrontery I swear that our new belle—the *Countess* de Courville as she brazenly calls herself, is naught but a tavern doxy turned lady! The saucy minx is an imposter for I first encountered her in very different guise to her fine feathers. I speak true for I met her scarce a month or two back, plying for trade at The Crown Tavern Bordello in Cheapside!"

An audible gasp went up as appalled listeners turned

126

to stare at the new favorite. Sir Michael went white with anger and would have held Camilla's hand more closely, but she wrenched it free and stood up, facing Sir Caspar with flashing eyes:

"How dare you, Sir? I will not deny our first meeting but, since you were too far gone in wine to stand, I swear your memory is grievously at fault! Far from wishing your advances I repelled them with all my strength—and I am no imposter. Proudly I claim my right to the title I hold and you . . . . you . . ." Emotion overcame her, rising in great waves of nausea and despair until they almost choked her. With the inarticulate cry of a helplessly trapped young animal, she turned and sped before even Sir Michael realized what was happening.

Blinded as she was by tears of enraged humiliation, she ran desperately through the crowded room toward the doors as the word *"Imposter"* rang in her ears, passed avidly from those closest to the dramatic scene to people seated at tables further away.

Sir Michael rose and started in hot pursuit of his love, only, by then, his progress was sorely impeded as elegant members of the *ton* had also risen, determined to give the disgraceful news to friends who might not have heard the exchange.

Camilla reached the grand hall unmolested; by then the tears were flowing freely down her cheeks, but her heart was weeping for the imagined betrayal of her love, Sir Michael.

"Oh, Michael—my dearest, my heart—I have marred your honor, ruined you—and the pain is more than I can bear!"

Two flunkeys, dozing quietly in the hall, started to their feet in owlish astonishment as the proclaimed beauty of the evening demanded, through racking sobs:

"I must have air—pray where is the nearest door?"

Thinking her to have taken ill, one politely showed her the way to the ladies powder closet, but, as she looked wildly around she saw the great deserted ballroom and, at the end, a blessedly open French window.

As Sir Michael reached the hall, Camilla was already out in a small, paved garden set around with ornamental shrubs. Disregarding her beautiful white gown, she crept behind one of the shrubs for shelter and there, huddled close against the wall, strove to overcome her tears before running further.

Oh, if only she had spoken of her past to Sir Michael as their relationship developed! It was certainly not from shame, since she loved her foster-mother dearly—no, she had been too eager to please him with her newfound knowledge of the arts and so hold his interest. Now it would all come out in a manner most harmful to his honor and prestige as he heard her story secondhand— how desperately he must, even now, be regretting his avowal of love! This thought was like a sword in her heart —she should not have accepted his noble offer so readily, should have warned him that he did not yet know enough about her and, only when she had told him all and given him the chance to change his mind, would she have been gladly, freely able to reveal her heart.

Now it was all too late—through his viciousness, Sir Caspar had laid her finest evening, her dreams, and the love of her life in ruins.

Suddenly. she heard Sir Michael's voice at the open windows:

"Countess Camilla! *Countess*—pray answer me if you are here!"

In reality his voice was filled with deep concern but, in her dire plight, it sounded sharp, reproving, and she cringed still more closely against the wall where she could not possibly be visible.

When no answer came after a few moments he returned to the ballroom and, as his handsome figure disappeared from view, Camilla bade him a heartbroken, silent farewell, pledging him her eternal love knowing she might never see him again.

As she felt her way cautiously toward a gate she could not know how deeply she had underrated the staunchness and courage of Sir Michael. Indeed, he cared not a fig for her past as he strode purposefully back to the now up-roarious supper room determined to challenge Caspar Randal in front of all—challenge him to provide proof of his outrageous statements.

Once outside the garden, Camilla found herself in a well-kept passageway running behind the grand mansions to give access for certain tradesmen. There was only one thought in her mind: to reach the comforting arms of her dearest mama, Mrs. Fernaby, whose love and understanding had never failed. She was far too distracted to remember how unsuitably clad she was to venture, at midnight, from the wealthy West End to Cheapside for she had not even spared the time to fetch her cloak.

As she started to run in the all-too-familiar direction, Sir Michael found that he was not without strong support for his love's good name. Not only the Marquise rose to join him, but Mrs. Fitzherbert herself, curious about the raised voices, had emerged from the private dining room where she sat with the prince. The Marquise laid a detaining hand on Sir Michael's arm as he made toward Sir Caspar:

"No—no, Sire. Rather escort me immediately to my house where we shall certainly find Camilla and where my dear husband has irrefutable proof of her lineage. Imposter, indeed!" she added with icy scorn. Mrs. Fitzherbert added her advice:

"'Tis a wise course, Sir Michael—I declare I have seen the title deeds myself and that villain, Randal, can have no accusation to level at the girl we all hold so dear!"

Quelling his urgent desire to catch Randal by the throat if need be, Sir Michael agreed to find his Camilla, to take her tenderly, reassuringly in his arms, ousted all else. He and the Marquise left with all speed.

Meantime Camilla, half-crazed with grief, had reached the highway, crossed it and darted, wraithlike in her

129

white gown, into a familiar byway. Soon, soon she would feel the loving arms of Hannah Fernaby cradling her close against her heart in defiant protection from even the most mortal blows of Fortune.

As he left the supper room, Sir Michael called clearly to Sir Caspar: "I shall call you out on the morrow, sir. Be ready!"

Chapter Nine

It was a perilous thing, in any event, for a young lady of fashion in a rich ballgown to hasten, unaccompanied, to the East End of London. But in Camilla's case it was made worse by a brilliant full moon now at its zenith in the calm night sky, lighting all the lanes from directly overhead. In her headlong flight no thought of snatching up a cloak or any other dark covering had crossed her mind and, even now, she was unaware of her shimmering figure gleaming like an opal in the silver light.

One or two men, lurching rather uncertainly toward home after a drinking bout, made to seize at her arm or catch her by the skirts, but she swiftly wrenched herself free with no thought of personal danger. Her mind was totally filled by Michael—of her hopeless sense of guilt, although her deception of him had been in no way deliberate. Unaware of the bitter malice of Sir Caspar and the greed of Thomas Fernaby, infinite time had seemed to stretch ahead during which she and Michael would talk in peace, holding no secrets.

Now it was too late. Indeed she would write to him—pour out her heart in self-accusation—but never, never again would she see his dear face, trusting and on fire with love.

Her legs were tiring and the almost forgotten stench of the mean East End alleyways sickened her; but since she must be within a mile or less of The Crown, Camilla spurred her efforts. Soon she could rest in the familiar kitchen with Mrs. Fernaby's affection spreading a cloak of comfort around her as they talked together over strong, hot tea.

Her mind was so filled with this wonderful picture that she did not notice four figures emerging from a dark passage on her right. Indeed, their every movement was stealthy and, on seeing the visionary girl running alone toward them they waited, staring. Then their leader muttered something under his breath and, as Camilla was almost past them she was suddenly seized from behind, both arms pinioned behind her back.

Startled and outnumbered as she was, she struggled like a wild thing to free herself, twisting and turning her slender body until the grip on her arms tightened so painfully she gasped for breath. Through a mist of agony she was aware of being hustled down a dark tunnel, then thrust through a door behind which the only faint flicker of light came from a fire that had died to embers.

There was no sound save heavy breathing for a moment, then a faint movement as someone must have lit a taper from the embers and caused a small wick in oil to cast fitful light and shadow around the desolate room.

Camilla strained her eyes to see her captors, but they were still behind her, not loosening their cruel hands. One only stood facing her, hands on hips, the face hawklike and bitter with one eye covered by a black patch from which a hideous scar ran down to the edge of a thin mouth. Amazed, Camilla realized that this was a woman and, a moment later, that she was the leader:

"Let 'er go," she commanded in a harsh low voice.

As the pressure left her arms the pain was even more acute until circulation returned. Then three men slouched around to join the woman and four pairs of black, gimlet eyes raked her from head to foot, assessing their prize. Defensively, Camilla clasped her bruised arms across her breast. Then one man guffawed:

132

"I say we 'ave some sport with 'er, eh."

"She asked for it," echoed another, but the woman stepped quickly in front of Camilla while her tongue lashed them:

"Fools!" she hissed. "We've got a pot o' gold this night —some la-di-dah gal worth 'er weight in gold sovereigns —more'n we earn in a lifetime o' petty pilfering. Ransom, me boys! So long as the goods be undamaged, and I'll flay ye alive if ye touch 'er! *Get out* and about yer night's business—ye can pleasure yerselves where ye please, but not 'ere. Tom"—she glanced at a slightly older man who had not joined the others in their lewd plans—"Get yer brothers out o' the place. We can do wi' some fine fat purses 'til we get yon ransom."

He proved to be surprisingly strong and muscular, and, while his brothers muttered and cursed at being baulked of their prey, he had them outside and the door slammed shut behind them.

The sudden silence was eerie. The woman did not move and Camilla saw that she was being held in a derelict kitchen with hardly any furniture; the walls were dark and peeling, the rusty range had an oven door hanging loose and the floor consisted of cold, uneven stone. In an alcove stood a bed of sorts on which filthy blankets were piled anyhow. She shivered since weariness, shock, and pain seemed to have frozen through to her very bones.

"May I . . . " she began tentatively, "may I go nearer the fire? I—I am very cold."

The woman went forward and grudgingly tossed a little fresh fuel on the embers:

"I s'pose so—don't want ye sick 'til yer grand family pay me price." She offered no chair or stool so Camilla huddled as close as she could to the tiny flicker that sprang up, crouched on the dirty floor. Her ballgown was already ruined and it brought such memories of heartbreak that she would never wear it again in any case.

The woman drew up a wooden chair and straddled it:

"Now—yer name?"

"Camilla." There was a pause. "May I know yours? I —I'm sorry about the scar, it looks painful."

It was the wrong thing to have said for the woman flared:

"No one pities Sal Perkins, me gal, least of all your sort! 'Twas one of yer fine *gentlemen* as did it. Now then, where d'ye come from?"

Camilla shivered more but said nothing. No matter what torture was inflicted on her she would die sooner than expose the elderly Marquis and Marquise de Fouchet to these swine.

Sal watched her steadily then shrugged. She fetched a vile blanket from the bed and flung it around Camilla's bare shoulders.

"Don't thank me," she growled, "I'm but protectin' me goods."

At first her skin revolted from contact with the rough, sour smelling material, but her need for warmth was too strong and, realizing that the blanket smelt no worse than the room, Camilla drew it more closely around her. Sal Perkins resumed the chair.

"Get yer wits together, gal," she commanded. "The sooner ye tell us yer dad's name the sooner ye'll be free." She gave a twisted smile "Or mebbe 'tis some fancy man who dressed ye up like a grand lady and had yer hair done up so fine? It's naught to me—they'll pay just the same."

Camilla had been thinking as carefully as she could. Now she raised her gray eyes and said:

"Send your message to Mrs. Fernaby at The Crown Tavern. *She's* my mother, I declare, and she'll deal with your demands."

Sal's laughter was an ugly sound: "Hannah *Fernaby?* 'Strewth, her Thomas keeps 'er skint for a penny! And how d'yer know 'er name? Were yer one of the doxies workin' there and caught yerself a fine, rich fish, eh?"

Camilla flinched at the loathsome word that had already ruined her life.

134

"I most certainly was *not*," she retorted with spirit. "I am telling the truth—Hannah Fernaby has always been *my mother!*" She knew that she was placing Mrs. Fernaby in no danger for Hannah was both wise and wily about the world of the East End—she had many friends, powerful ones, and if only she knew of Camilla's plight and her wherabouts all might be solved.

"Pray send word to her," she pleaded.

Sal Perkins obviously did not consider this worth answering. Instead she said:

"Be a fool then, if it pleases yer. I'll 'ave ter send word out all over the West End and it won't be first time, neither. Times we've come by some rich bauble as we couldn't sell 'round these parts—but the owner was mighty glad to pay full price and more. Me boy'll be 'ere any time now—works the lanes by night, then scrubs up like an angel and 'e and 'is pals be fine messenger boys in the West End all mornin', carryin' flowers and sich to the gentry. Fair spread the word they do *and* get results! So, if that's how yer want it ye leave me no choice."

Momentarily, Camilla panicked—what if such a message were delivered to the Marquise? Then her heart sank to new depths—No one, no one in the whole world after hearing Caspar Randal's taunt, would care what became of her now. Only Mrs. Fernaby would remain staunch, knowing the truth. All the others would believe her to be a countess, possibly, but a woman of ill-repute, most certainly . . . a traitor to her class.

Oh, if only, if *only* her whereabouts could be known!

At that very moment Sir Michael Monford was pacing the floor of the Marquis de Fouchet's library like a caged tiger while the old man and his wife sat white-faced, longing to help him:

"But since Camilla is not here—where *can* she be?" Sir Michael urged. "She cannot have vanished!"

135

Slowly the Marquise recollected her wits, shattered by the scene at the Royal Ball:

"I fancy she may have gone to a Mrs. Fernaby who lives at The Crown Tavern in Cheapside. That good woman brought up Camilla after her poor mother died and, until Fouchet found her, the girl called Mrs. Fernaby 'Mama,' believing it to be the truth. I warrant they loved each other dearly. Yes, I think she has gone there."

Sir Michael was appalled: "In a ballgown—to the East End? Why, she will be in danger at every step! The Crown, did you say?"

The Marquise nodded assent.

For a moment the distraught young man put a hand over his eyes as memories flooded over him: he saw, again, the beautiful girl beating off the drunken advances of Caspar Randal with all her strength, then kneeling at his own side as they gathered the shards from a broken jar of grog—her concern over his stained hose—her low, musical voice as they talked; finally, which now pierced him to the heart, the way he had spurned her most cruelly on the appearance of her wicked foster-father! And all the time this had been his most beloved, precious Camilla whom pride told him then that he must not love since she was but a low-born tavernkeeper's daughter. No wonder he had searched London for a replica of her lovely face until he found it. Shame and self-loathing swept through him for surely she must share those memories, have recognized him long ago, and yet not one word of reproach ever crossed her lips.

And that, of course, was the basis on which Randal had built tonight's evil accusation at the ball!

Sir Michael suddenly realized that the old Marquis had risen from his chair—was speaking, and holding out some parchment:

". . . I am remiss, these are the deeds, Sir Michael, the deeds that prove Camilla's entitlement."

"I do not need them! Why, her every look, thought,

136

and word proclaim her nobility without need of written proof! Pray forgive me—I have tarried too long and I must be off to The Crown with Godspeed!" He hastened to the door, turning only to say "I thank you both with all my heart . . . I will bring news." And he was gone.

A flunkey sprang to attention as Sir Michael rushed into the hall, calling:

"My carriage! 'Twill be near Carlton House, call it immediately."

In the distance Camilla heard the watch cry: "Three o' the clock and All's Well!" and it revived her flagging courage—there must be a main highway nearby—Holborn, perhaps where, if she could only escape she might seek refuge with Mrs. Fernaby's uncle, the pawnbroker. This faint glimmer of hope brought her thoughts into clear focus for they had wandered a little between chill and drowsiness during the past hour.

I am alone, she thought clearly, for not a soul in the West End will offer to ransom me—why should they? And so, if need be, I must fight my way through to Mrs. Fernaby.

Sal startled her by speaking abruptly after a long silence during which she had sat motionless:

"I'll have that gown off ye afore ye filthy it more, me gal. Remove it!"

"I will not," retorted Camilla. "I declare I have but a fine shift and a petticoat beneath it and I refuse to face your hateful men in such undress."

Sal stood up, laughing without mirth:

"Ye must think I've lost me wits! Nay, they'll scarce know ye when I'm done! Now, *take it off!* Ye're dad or ye're fancy man'll not care if ye're in calico when they git yer back, but yon gown be worth a sovereign I reckon and I mean to have it."

"What if I still refuse?"

" 'Twill go badly for ye—I'll whip it off ye!" Sal was in a rage so Camilla, still testing her newfound mettle, replied demurely:

"Then, surely, I shall be 'damaged goods'—no man will pay your demands if there are welts on my skin!"

Sal swore heartily and went to the bed, dragging something from under the sagging mattress. Swinging around she held up a garment shaped more like a tent than a dress in a gray, coarse material much creased: *"If ye were reared at The Crown, I'll swear ye've worn worse in yer time!"*

So it was a test. Perchance if she donned the loathsome thing Sal Perkins might believe her at last, Camilla thought, and send for Mrs. Fernaby. Suppressing her shuddering distaste, she began slowly, and with some difficulty since the Marquise's French maid had assisted her before—Camilla tried to undo the fastenings. Sal grew impatient, shouting:

" 'Ere—I'm not waitin' all night!" as she roughly tore the tiny silken buttons and small hooks loose. Then she dragged the lovely gown over Camilla's head.

The stiff calico was as unpleasant as she had feared, prickling over her bare arms and shoulders, but Camilla gave no sign.

"Now will you believe that I was reared at The Crown?"

But Sal was too engrossed in valuing the exquisite gown that lay in her roughened hands—if a wistful touch of longing softened her face for a moment Camilla did not see it for 'twas gone in a moment.

Then a gentle but insistent scratching noise came from outside the door and instantly the gown was bundled into a shadowy corner as Sal hastened to pull back the heavy bolt, and turn the key.

The Crown Tavern was in total darkness as Sir Michael left his carriage, and his heart sank. Surely if Camilla, by

138

a miracle, had reached her old home unscathed, there should be one light at least. But urgency drove him on and he went down the side alley and into the yard leading to the back door. Blackness everywhere. Then he saw the outside stair to the attic and, refusing defeat, he stood on the bottom stair and called up in a loud whisper:

"Mrs. Fernaby! *Mrs. Fernaby!* Are you there?"

At first nothing stirred; then, cautiously, the wooden latch shifted and the door swung open as a woman called in a low voice:

"Who calls at this hour?"

"Sir Michael Monford—I call most urgently about your foster-daughter, the Countess de Courville!" His tone was equally subdued, not wishing to wake Thomas Fernaby.

Without further ado, Mrs. Fernaby hurried down the stairs, her face pale and anxious in the light of the waning moon as she clutched his arm.

"She—she has come to no harm?"

"I do not know," he replied gravely. "May we go inside?"

With a movement of her head she signalled him to follow her as she swiftly found the key, opened the kitchen door, and went ahead of him to light the candle.

He closed the door carefully behind him.

"So—she is not here?" he asked.

"Why no! Tonight was to be the night of her life, she told me, she was bid to the Royal Ball. Oh, sir, pray tell me what has befallen—you look so pale. Pray sit ye down."

But Sir Michael could not rest. He paced the kitchen as he had paced the Marquis' library, his fears for Camilla now greater than ever.

Hannah Fernaby listened without interruption as he related all the events leading up to her flight.

"We had expressed our mutual love, the Countess and I," ended Sir Michael, "when, during supper, Sir Caspar Randal voiced his infamous scandal! She replied, hotly—

139

but then she fled . . . no one knows where." His handsome face was suddenly exhausted as he added: "You are my last hope, Mrs. Fernaby, for since she is not here, some terrible mishap must have overtaken her . . . she waited for no cloak but ran out in a glorious white and gold ballgown!"

With a face as drawn and ashen as his own, Mrs. Fernaby had nevertheless set the kettle over the banked up fire.

"Headstrong, my little Camilla—always has been," she said, "and fearless—must be her breedin'. But there is naught more ye can do, Sir Michael, pray believe me, this part o' London has no use fer gentlemen—if ye'll pardon me, but 'tis true. I'll warrant she must have been kidnapped—held fer ransom by some rascally band who haunt these streets after dark. If I'm right ye'll have news of her in the morning, I swear." Then she reconsidered: "No, 'twill be more likely afternoon." For she, like Sal Perkins, knew something of the messenger boys, though she'd had no cause to use them so far.

"Afternoon!" Sir Michael looked appalled. "That gentle, fragile girl to be held in some den of villains so long? What may they not do to her?"

"Naught—if she be fer ransom, rest assured, Sir." Hannah managed a little smile in an attempt to comfort him. "She'll be well cared for, I swear it—and my Camilla has great spirit and fine mettle in her, believe me. Now may I suggest you go home, Sir Michael? For I must go out this very minute—there's no time to be lost."

"Can I truly be of no service?" he asked, since he longed to be out and about in these mean alleys, seeking and defending his dear love by the sword if need be. To wait like a cowardly poltroon went against all his noble instincts.

Hannah Fernaby understood something of this turmoil: "I know 'tis hard for a brave gentleman deep in love, Sir, but pray, pray believe me when I say that your intervention 'round these parts could place Camilla in sore danger.

140

Waiting may be irksome but 'tis the way you'll best help her."

Grudgingly, he knew she was right and, ungraciously for him, he took his leave.

"Save her, Mistress Fernaby. I will offer rewards—ransom—anything demanded so that she be restored to me!"

Mrs. Fernaby smiled sadly after him, then hastened to don her skirt, bodice, and shawl which she kept in the kitchen for, since Thomas had grown more abusive, she often did not ascend to the attic at all. As she let herself out of the back door she prayed fervently:

"Pray God my lass be safe—and kindly treated."

Like a wraith she slipped away into the darkness.

Camilla strained to hear what passed between Sal Perkins and her expected visitor, but the conversation was carried on in a low whisper and quite inaudible.

So she turned her mind back to the remote chance of escape: the window offered most possibility although it was small and set shoulder-high in the wall; but a rusty latch was still inside and, striving to forget her sore, bruised arms, Camilla felt certain that by reaching up and exerting all her strength she might push the window outward. It certainly led only into the dark alley and, easing her way through, she might land on her head so she set herself to consider how to avoid this mishap. The stiff calico dress would prove troublesome, too, whereas her silken gown might have eased her passage.

But such plans were useless unless Sal left her alone for at least a few minutes and the woman showed no sign of any such thing. Indeed, returning from the rebolted door, her scarred face looked quite triumphant:

"The boy tells me as there'll be big trade in flowers to be delivered this morning after a Royal Ball . . . many sent to ye no doubt by wealthy ninnies!" she sneered. "So

141

ye're wastin' me time hidin' yer address under yer petti-coats! But I'll not hand ye over 'til me terms be met."

"How long will it be 'til your messenger returns?"

Sal shrugged. "Midday, mebbe, mebbe later—but don't fancy as he'll lead yer man straight to me door! Oh, no! I have me arrangements."

Camilla's heart sank. If it were midday or worse, after-noon, before the message came saying that not one of the members of the *ton* were interested in paying a large sum for her release then she was doomed. Sal's husband and his lecherous brothers would be here in this loathsome room to hear the news and then. . . . She shrank from even contemplating the horror that would follow. She made her final plea:

"Will you not believe me and send word to Mrs. Fernaby? I swear that she will find the means to pay what you ask—pray, *pray* do so!"

"One thousand golden guineas?" Sal gave her mirthless laugh. "That woman can't lay 'er hand to a thousand pence!"

Sal began to stir a black iron pot on the back of the rusty range, then she drew it forward, adding a little fuel to the fire:

" 'Tis a right shame that sich as ye should take the food out o' our mouths, but when the money comes we'll 'ave good red meat an' more!"

Camilla was thankful for the added warmth from the fire but the odor given off by the pot revolted her. Still, she could not refuse this offer since, in spite of all her adventures, she was hungry.

As soon as a wisp of steam curled up, Sal seized an iron ladle and placed two helpings of broth into earthen-ware bowls. The spoon she passed to Camilla was of battered tin and none too clean but it was clearly a test—a test to prove whether Camilla had ever eaten in the East End before. If she passed this one, perchance Sal would send the message to Mrs. Fernaby.

Gingerly, Camilla took the first small mouthful . . . .

Driving home, his mind in ferment, Sir Michael ordered his coachman to make a detour into Carlton Terrace. The Marquis might still be awake and eager to hear of his conversation with Mrs. Fernaby. It would be a relief to talk away some of the terrible hours that stretched ahead since sleep was to him quite out of the question.

There were many lights, indeed, not only one. So Sir Michael went quickly to the front door and was admitted.

The Marquis and Marquise still sat in the library, almost as they had done when he left except that the Marquise had since changed from her superb evening gown into a peignoir of delicate pink and white lace ruffles.

They both looked up with eager eyes as Sir Michael came in.

"Did you find Camilla?" asked the Marquis.

"Alas, no. She has not been seen at The Crown."

"Then she must have met with disaster!" cried the Marquise, starting out of her chair. "Oh, Camilla, dearest girl . . ." she swayed and sank down again, her breath coming fast. "Fouchet—my smelling bottle, pray, I fear I shall swoon."

The Marquis hurried to obey while Michael went to the side table where decanters and glasses were always set ready for a nightcap. He poured a small measure of brandy which, when she had recovered a little from the aid of the smelling bottle, he persuaded her to sip.

"Forgive me, I entreat you—for Mrs. Fernaby is not without hope and comfort. She swears that Camilla is being held by rogues for ransom and she was going out immediately to make inquiries. I have told her that I will pay *anything*—my whole fortune if need be, to ensure the safety of my love. I begged to stay with her—to assist if possible, but Mrs. Fernaby refused." He gave a wry smile. "It seems the gentry are unwelcome in the East End, but 'tis hard indeed to feel so helpless when so much is at stake!"

"I warrant Mrs. Fernaby is right, tho'—did she say when she would have news?"

"By midday, but it will more likely be afternoon before any word comes."

"So long!" murmured the Marquise whose heart still pained her a little. "I shall spend each long hour at my prie Dieu, praying the Good Lord to have mercy and save the precious child unharmed."

"Will you not rest, my dear?" pleaded her anxious husband. "I swear it will break Camilla's heart if you become ill on her behalf. Pray allow me to summon Marie who will help you to bed—there will still be many hours in the morning for your prayers which will be joined by my own."

"And mine," Sir Michael added forcefully, then wisely held his own counsel: of what use to speak his thoughts aloud to the old couple? His passionate longing to give Camilla's captors a taste of his sword—to ride his noble stallion, Spartacus, into their midst and fell them down before riding away with his dear love rescued and clasped against his heart in front of the saddle. But these were valiant dreams, whereas he knew, in his rebellious heart, that Mrs. Fernaby's way was right: her love for the beautiful captive was almost as great as his own and, like a lioness protecting her young, she would discover where Camilla was being held.

"I fear I have brought sad tidings, Marquise." He lifted her small hand and kissed it gallantly. "But I entreat you take your husband's advice and rest a little, since Mrs. Fernaby inspires great confidence. I vow *she* will not rest until Camilla is found and the only aid we can offer is patience, hard tho' it be. I will be here in the morning to wait until word comes."

With a formal bow to the Marquis he took his leave, knowing that he would have neither rest nor sleep that night.

The first streaks of dawn crept dimly through the high, cobwebbed window in Sal Perkins' kitchen and Camilla

144

felt her courage falter: it surely meant that the men would return before long, their night's work done—then her slender chances of escape would be doomed. With them present to watch—and possibly violate her—it would matter not if Sal left the place for a time.

And it was at that low point that a seeming miracle occurred: Sal rose off the hard chair she had occupied throughout the night, stretched, and went to a small door at the side of the old range:

"No fancy tricks, mind! Ye can't open the door for I've the key in me pocket—besides, the yard beyond be small and I can hear every move ye make!"

Regardless of this warning, all Camilla's strength came flooding back. Sal must be going outside to pump water and, from her own experience, Camilla knew that it took at least five minutes to fill a few pails. It was the answer to her prayers!

The moment Sal disappeared, leaving the small door wide, she rose from her cramped position by the fire and, stiffness forgotten, crossed swiftly to the old window . . . .

Chapter Ten

Long before the first signs of dawn, Mrs. Fernaby slipped quietly through the back streets that surrounded The Crown Tavern, her dark, shawled figure unmolested, for no rogue, however dark his deeds, would interfere with Hannah Fernaby.

She came to a two-storey house that had seen better days and made her way down the area steps to the back door. It was, as ever, unlocked and the latch well-oiled so that it opened silently.

Inside, beside a bright fire, old Ma Hewitt sat in a rocking chair, moving back and forth in perfect rhythm. No one had ever seen her otherwise, day or night, and rumor had it that she never slept for, although she never broke the law herself, her house was a refuge at any hour for vagabonds and villains who wished to lie low.

She welcomed Hannah with real pleasure:

"Why, my dear, come ye in and welcome—if that wicked man o' yours has beaten ye once too often ye'll be safe here."

Mrs. Fernaby smiled. "No, no—'tis not Thomas, Ma—'tis a matter much closer to my heart. My dear foster-daughter has been kidnapped 'round these parts I reckon, she'll be held for ransom."

Ma Hewitt's small eyes sharpened. "Yon pretty wench ye called Camilla? I liked her right well. I remember—

146

a sweet child—but who would steal her from under ye're very nose? And for why?"

Hannah shook her head and, as briefly as she could, outlined the new turn Camilla's life had taken over the past three months.

"So there she was, driven half out o' her mind with grief, running from yon Grand Ball given by the prince himself, to seek comfort with me. In the grandest gown ye ever did see, I'm told." She hesitated, then added simply, "Always knew she'd turn to me in trouble. Oh, Ma, I'm half crazed meself with worry—have ye heard aught?"

The old woman shook her head, drawing her thin lips in over toothless gums as she considered the crisis.

"What reward's offered fer information, dear?"

Hannah considered the coins left on her table by Sir Michael as he left, now carefully hidden deep in the flour jar where Thomas would never look.

"Say, a guinea fer you and one fer whoever brings news?"

Ma Hewitt nodded. " 'Tis fair enough I be reckoning." After all she had a good heart but she was not a charity and she took commission from her messengers as well, so it was worth her while.

"I'll put it about, Hannah, and if there's news I'll send to ye tomorrow—midday mebbe." Without interrupting her rocking she poked the fire to even greater warmth. "Now ye'd best be goin'—I'm expectin' company later and they'll not want to find ye here!" she chuckled. "They be night folk and secret."

Hannah left, her heart a deal lighter, for the old woman's network spread wide and 'twas not often she was paid in guineas. As Mrs. Fernaby's soft footsteps receded up the area steps, Ma Hewitt awaited two nightly visitors in particular: one, an expert pickpocket who worked the taverns and he, if anyone, would know where Camilla was held. The other, a fresh-faced lad of fifteen, who committed petty thefts by night then turned messenger boy

147

for a West End florist by day. Ma knew perfectly well that all the lads in the area worked together when information was needed but she usually arranged payment so that the news reached her first, giving her a good lead in the reward stakes.

Meantime, alone in Sal's kitchen, Camilla worked fast for there was little time. Her arms protested when she raised them to the rusty window latch, but desperation gave her strength whereby she could ignore pain—to be free at last, hastening to her dear mama, spurred her on. Time later to give way to the countless aches and bruises.

Holding her breath she raised the latch and pushed—to no avail. Drawing a deep breath she redoubled her effort and was rewarded by a grinding, creaking movement as the rotten latch gave way under the pressure. She paused, terrified, to listen: had the sound, slight though it was, carried out to Sal Perkins? But Fate was on her side, Camilla felt thankfully, as at that very moment she could hear water gushing from the pump. She pushed harder still and the window swung outward.

Only it was too high. She must fetch the upright chair to stand on before she could push her slender body through the blessed opening, yet Sal must be almost finished outside. The pump gushed harder, as though being used in a hurry.

Camilla ran across, seized the chair and, in what amounted to frenzy, mounted it and grasped the rotten window sill. Her head and shoulders passed through easily and she remembered to shift her grip from inside to the outer sill so that, with luck, she might twist around and drop feet first instead of on her head.

But the calico dress was both stiff and voluminous and seemed to have gathered around her hips—but she refused defeat now, when half her body was through and free and her gasps drew in great draughts of dawn air.

148

One more supreme effort, she thought, and exerted all her strength.

Then her heart stopped. Claw-like hands had her by the ankles and, with vicious speed that grazed her sorely, Camilla was dragged back into captivity. Sal was so angry that her scar showed livid against a pale face:

"Ye misbegotten little cheat!" hissed the husky voice. "Thought to trick me, eh?" She flung Camilla away with such force that the girl sprawled on the stone floor and there lay still as renewed pain washed over her and her eyes filled with the scalding tears of anguished disappointment. Sal stood over her.

"I've a mind to let me brothers-in-law 'ave their way! Ye're fancy man willna know the difference, and 'twould be fair punishment, I'm thinkin'."

At that Camilla pushed herself up with some difficulty. "No—no, I pray you, you can't do that!" She gathered the shreds of her near-broken courage; that nightmare would be her lot, undoubtedly, when no ransom was offered for her, but not yet—not yet. "I shall tell him instantly if you have had me violated!" she flared. "Then you'll be hounded by the law, I swear it!"

The point went home, although Sal threw back her head and laughed proudly, "Ye think the law'll ever find Sal Perkins? Not on yer life," she scoffed. But she knew it was just possible—Sal was a well-known figure in this world of hers and if good money was offered she could not trust her so-called friends and accomplices.

"Very well," she conceded reluctantly. "I'll protect ye 'til me lad brings news—'ere, cover yer hair wi' this and dirty yer face . . . ashes'll do."

Gratefully, Camilla tied an old gray rag over her still bright hair and eagerly smeared her forehead and cheeks. Sal surveyed the results, satisfied: "Now huddle down like an old crone and make no move when they come in—they'll be drunken anyways."

Camilla obeyed just in time, drawing the blanket that

149

lay still where she had dropped it on the hearth, as closely as she could up around her aristocratic jawline.

The men came in with much uproar, laughing, and making lewd jokes as they, perforce, spilled out the night's takings for Sal's approval. Of the muffled figure they took no notice at all.

Sal was terse:

"Poor pickin's ye've got, in truth—scarce five sovereigns and a mort o' useless baubles. Get to bed afore ye fall down! Tom?"

As his brothers tumbled into the bed, her husband came to her side and Camilla could hear that he was sober:

"Where's the gal, wife?"

"Here." There was a note of triumph in her voice. "Tried to escape through yon old window—but I was too quick!"

"D'ye truly think as we'll get the money?" he asked.

"O' *course* we will! She's a right beauty and no mistake, some rich fool must want her bad."

They moved out of earshot, talking in undertones as Sal outlined the plans she had given to her messenger.

Camilla's mind strayed, treacherously, back to her beloved Sir Michael . . . she imagined him receiving the "message" from her kidnappers with a stony glance of repudiation. *Oh, Michael, Michael, my own true love,* she whispered, *unable even now that dawn had come, to accept that my own foolishness had robbed me of all happiness.* Silently, she began to cry.

Could she only have known the true facts, Camilla's heart would have been high, for the people she held most dear knew no sleep that night.

Sir Michael impatiently paced up and down, through the hall, library, and dining room of his house in Curzon Street, willing the hours to pass. His sister Augusta, almost as distressed as he, tried to keep him company but, by three A.M. was forced to surrender to sleep. Her own

150

evening had been glorious with Brent Edwards finally confessing his love which she most ardently reciprocated. Furthermore, he had shown great sensitivity over the disaster that had befallen her brother and her dear friend, the young Countess.

"I will place myself at his disposal," Mr. Edwards declared. "It will be a pleasure to act as his Second if he calls out that rascal, Randal, to a duel!"

But, as she thankfully succumbed to sleep, Augusta knew that her brother would take no such steps until news of his beloved came.

The Marquis de Fouchet made no attempt to sleep. After his dear wife had retired to the ministrations of her maid, he sat on in the library reliving his eternal love for Claudette de Courville whose very image had come back into his life through her lovely grand-daughter. It was as though she had given him a sacred trust to protect and guide the girl, and now he had failed.

If he had only attended the ball instead of indulging his passion for privacy, he might have prevented the disaster —or, at least, restrained Camilla in her flight.

While, at The Crown, Hannah Fernaby sat the night out in her kitchen, brooding, pondering whether there was more she might do to discover Camilla's whereabouts. She knew many petty thieves but none who would resort to kidnapping and Sal Perkins was in the Holborn area, as Camilla had guessed, and so not familiar around Cheapside.

That was where Ma Hewitt was so invaluable—her house lay midway between Cheapside and Holborn with Ludgate Hill to the South so she heard news from all quarters.

By six o'clock Sir Michael could bear it no longer. Since no message was possible before midday, he would ride— ride hard to quell the restlessness in his heart, for waiting was anathema to a man of action. He was irked, also, because he could not fulfill his threat and call out Caspar Randal to a duel—not until he had definite news of

Camilla. His great love for her grew and deepened with each hour that passed.

But if waiting was testing for those who loved her, it was torture to Camilla. When her husband, Tom, lay down to doze beside his brothers, Sal grew edgy and ill-tempered, ordering Camilla to clear the ashes and sweep the hearth, believing that the girl would bungle it and so give her a chance to lash out with her tongue. Yet, as she watched, Camilla performed the dreary task neatly from long practice. When Sal sneered, Camilla smiled sweetly.

"I have done such work since childhood for my mother at The Crown!" This drove her point home neatly and she could see that Sal was wondering, impatiently, if she had been wrong not to send word to Hannah Fernaby after all.

However, the worst thing for both of them was that there was no timepiece in the still-dark kitchen and it was nigh impossible to judge by the sun for it reached the narrow passage outside with difficulty and became filtered to only sickly light through the dust-grimed window.

"It *must* be midday," said Camilla desperately after a long, drawn-out, uneasy silence.

It was, indeed, as the others waiting so anxiously were aware, but the hour came and went with no news.

Hannah Fernaby incurred her husband's ready wrath by dropping a tankard in the sink; the Marquise drove de Fouchet to distraction by the constant opening and clicking shut of her fan. While in Curzon Street, Augusta Monford was hard put to know what to do with her brother: his ride had eased him not at all, and now he had resumed his endless pacing about the ground floor. It was nigh on three o'clock when the front door knocker thundered and a footman went to open it. Outside stood a lad in messenger's livery, studded with small brass buttons, his arms filled with flowers addressed to Miss Augusta. Handing them over the boy added, "I've a message fer every household, too. 'Tis none of me own doing, just a message ye know . . ."

152

Sir Michael, in the hall, strode forward. "What is it? I would know most urgently."

"Why, 'tis said as there's a rich lass fer ransom—I know not where," he added hastily with a most innocent expression. "The price be a thousand guineas and if so be ye've lost a relative, I'm to tell the rest."

"Tell me immediately!"

"Ye're to send a carriage and the money to Charing Cross this evenin' at six-thirty when the lass will be there, so the money be good."

"You need deliver your message no further," cried Sir Michael, bringing a half sovereign from his purse and giving it to the boy. "The carriage shall be there!"

The boy smirked and left. It was not part of his bargain that he should say he'd been paid better by a gentleman elsewhere.

In high excitement, Sir Michael told Augusta who had also come to the hall, the flowers being for her. Ignoring the lovely bouquets in her arms, her brother hugged her in his sudden exuberance—an embrace not bestowed since they were very small and she had unwillingly given up a favorite sweetmeat.

"I must go at once to the de Fouchets," he confided, "since they may not have had the glorious news! Oh, Augusta—she is *safe,* my dear love will be with us before dusk!"

The elderly couple were grateful indeed. The Marquise took the young man into her small, frail arms as though he were a son. "My dear, I am so happy I know not what to say! Pray, pray bring the poor child straight to us since she will have suffered much, I fear."

De Fouchet offered his hand in a warm grasp. "Charing Cross, eh? 'Tis a lonely enough spot, I warrant, the villains will get away scot free, but 'tis no matter if Camilla is unharmed."

The news travelled a trifle more slowly to the East End, for the messengers had had a splendid day but, at a quarter-to-four, the same scratching sound that had come

153

in the early hours, alerted both Sal and Camilla, who started up eagerly.

But, as before, she heard nothing of what passed at the door, only seeing from Sal's face that, by some miracle, the ransom was to be paid!

"Ye'll be leavin' us at five o' the clock," said Sal with more than a touch of triumph. "Yer rich fool o' a man will pay me price!"

"Oh," Camilla could say no more, her heart was so full: a *man* was offering the outrageous price! Who else could it be Sir Michael? Her pulse beat fast—even if he only wished to chastise her for her secrecy—rescind his declarations of love, at least she was to see him again, to hear his dear voice and be able to explain a little for her dilatory confession.

Ma Hewitt had the news at four and, true to her word, sent the lad straight to Hannah Fernaby who, she declared, would reward him handsomely. For it so happened that this very messenger had met with success. Indeed, the ransom money had been doubled.

Mrs. Fernaby was in her kitchen when the boy arrived and she drew him swiftly inside.

"You bring news of my daughter, Camilla?"

"Indeed, yes, Mistress—so you pay me me reward," he added cheekily.

Thankful in her very bones, Hannah gave him a whole sovereign, twice as much as any lad had received so far.

"Sit ye down," she cried, "and ye shall have one o' me rock cakes so ye tell me the whole story!"

For a golden guinea he would have told anything and, as he munched on the warm rock cake he did.

" 'Twas a handsome young gentleman," he began and her heart lifted: in answer to her fervent prayers surely he was Sir Michael? "Lives in Chambers," the boy went on. "Mighty grand an' all—fact, he must have been pretty anxious about yon lass since he came out to the hall and dismissed the servant to hear me 'isself." He hesitated a moment.

154

"Go on—go on—what message did you give?"

Wariness crept into the wide blue eyes—the lad was but fifteen and a long, profitable future stretched ahead if he betrayed no secret.

"The one given me," he answered stolidly. "I canna tell ye more, mistress."

"No, of course not," retorted Hannah in her most practical voice. "You lads do a great service, I know. But —since ye've had a good guinea, I wish to know the address o' this gentleman."

The boy turned the question over in his mind as he munched on his cake. Then he decided—the address of the monied man would not be of consequence to those that held the girl and Mrs. Fernaby looked quite capable of seizing back the precious gold coin.

" 'Twere number five, Albemarle Chambers—if I remember right," he mumbled.

"And where is she to be picked up?" Hannah's voice was sharp, for the address worried her. "Don't trifle wi' me, lad, I know these villains make a meeting place!"

He opened his innocent eyes wide. "I dinna know, Mistress, honest! Another boy goes to fix that."

Hannah gave a heavy sigh—that it was not true, she knew, but the boy had given her enough value for the guinea—at least in his own mind. For he would receive much more later.

Thanking the good Lord that Thomas was out, Hannah took down her shawl and set off briskly for Carlton Terrace.

Camilla was pleading with a much-better-tempered Sal:

"Pray, even if I may not have my own gown, at least allow me to wash at your pump? I—I declare I'll not face my noble rescuer besmirched with ashes!"

Grudgingly, Sal agreed, although she accompanied Camilla into the small yard. Having drawn a pailful, Camilla rinsed her face and arms again and again in the blessed, cold water, glad that she needed neither powder nor patches. But her hair! 'Twas in a sorry state, the tendrils bedraggled and the curls on top in great disarray after the rough way Sal had dragged off her ballgown.

"Have—have you a comb, by any chance?" she asked hopefully.

Sal stared at her, her own hair matted and filthy. "And what would I want wi' sich nonsense?" she answered scornfully. "Use yer fingers like other folk do!"

Camilla did her best but to not much avail, so she resolved to implore Sir Michael to give her a few moments to attend to her toilette before they talked.

In less than two hours from now she would be *free!*

Soon after five o'clock, two surly men arrived at the door, eyeing the girl they were to escort in a most unpleasant way.

" 'Ere—jist keep yer eyes ter yerself!" shouted Sal, angrily. Then, to Camilla: "Best cover yer head, lass, and pull it down over yer fore'ead." She tossed over the gray rag.

Camilla, frightened by the strangers, obeyed without demur.

Sal was giving her final instructions: "Five-thirty, sharp, mind. A carriage'll come and a man wi' the money—mind yer keep the lass 'til ye see the gold."

Meantime, Mrs. Fernaby was being admitted to the library where both de Fouchets rose eagerly to welcome her. Sir Michael was not present, which surprised her until she remembered that it was a man who had offered to pay the ransom. He must, even now, be awaiting Camilla's arrival.

Then, as she repeated word for word the message that had been brought to her, the Marquise exchanged a concerned, puzzled glance with her husband:

"But, Mrs. Fernaby," she said quickly, "we have always understood that Sir Michael has a fine house in Curzon

Street—indeed, it must be so since dear Camilla frequently visited his sister there."

A delicately ornate ormolu French clock on the mantlepiece already showed it to be five-fifteen and Hannah grew agitated. "Then there is little time—pray tell me the number and I will hasten to him. And yet . . ." she hesitated, "I cannot believe that any other gentleman would offer such a handsome sum for my daughter."

The Marquis pulled a bell-rope close to his hand. "I will order my carriage to be made ready instantly. 'Twill be around within ten minutes."

With strange fear mounting in her breast, Mrs. Fernaby was already by the door. "Thank you kindly, my lord, but 'twill be quicker on foot—running, if need be. The address, I pray."

The Marquise gave it with equal speed for she, too, was alarmed although she knew not why.

Camilla's unsavory escort marched her at a fine pace down side alleys to Ludgate Hill and thence up Fleet Street to The Strand. For once she had reason to be grateful to Sal Perkins since the men might well have proved dangerous had not one glanced over his shoulder and muttered:

"Devil take it! We've a hound on our tail—Tom Perkins and 'is brother!" Camilla had never thought to like any villain but Tom had spoken no unkind word to her and her heart warmed at his protection.

The Strand was full of grand mansions with gardens running down to the Thames at the back. Along the street were many vendors of fruit, flowers, and favors, still lingering for late custom. They paid no heed to two swarthy young men out walking with a drab—it was a common sight.

Charing Cross itself was deserted, just a stone cross surrounded by greensward that badly needed tending. But it was a spot where several roads converged and, since they were a trifle early, no carriage was yet in sight.

Camilla felt her longing mounting—if only Sir Michael had shown impatience—arrived early at the rendezvous—then despair seized her once again. Why should he behave like the eager lover any longer? His heart must be filled only with hatred and contempt.

They waited, the men talking together in undertones while Tom Perkins and his brother remained several yards off.

It took Hannah longer than she had hoped to reach Curzon Street for she twice missed her way and she was short of breath. But, at last, she came to the front door and hammered on the big knocker. It was a quarter to six. Sir Michael himself opened to her and his eyes widened in surprise:

"Why, Mistress Fernaby, come in. I am about to set out for Charing Cross where I am to meet my dear love at six-thirty. You wish to accompany me?"

"No, no, Sir, I'd not intrude in such a way. No—'tis the address as has me right anxious."

He drew her quickly inside and spoke almost harshly in his sudden urgency:

"What address is that? Surely the boy took mine plain enough?"

"It seems not, Sir." And she told him as briefly as she could the message that had come to her. His face darkened with anger and, even while she was speaking, he reached for his sword belt that always lay ready on a settle in the hall.

"I thank God, my carriage is due 'round. Come, Mistress Fernaby, and pray we are in time."

There was a short contretemps when the dark hired carriage drew up at Charing Cross and a burly man in servant's livery climbed down from the box beside the driver.

"You got the girl?" he asked.

158

"Aye, but 'tis cash first," said one of the escort. Camilla made to run to the carriage door, knowing Sir Michael must be inside, but the other man caught her arm roughly.

The servant shook his head. "My master be payin' twice yer price and he demands to see the goods first—he's offerin' for his cousin but if ye be passin' off another then ye'll get nowt."

Fortunately Camilla heard none of this since the two men had gone out of earshot toward Tom Perkins who had to be consulted. Seemingly, he reluctantly agreed to the terms—after all, no other rich fool had offered two thousand guineas for the wench. But he was uneasy, just the same, and gave instructions in a low voice: "Ye're to go wi' her—let 'im get a sight o' 'er at the door, then bring away the cash else 'twill go hard wi' ye, I swear it."

The man disliked this arrangement; it was not in his book to be seen—and possibly remembered—by some denizen of the West End. Or it could even be a plot by the law to trap the kidnappers. He demanded an exorbitant reward for the service and Tom Perkins was bound to give in . . . for him to go himself was impossible since, if it proved to be a trick his Sal would be left at the mercy of his brothers.

A few minutes later Camilla was pushed toward the carriage door, surprised to see the blinds drawn down, but quite certain that it was only Sir Michael's way of not being recognized on the drive. She stepped in, her mouth half open to cry his name . . . .

The musty interior was empty and, worse still, her escort crowded in behind her. Nervous, yet still trusting, she huddled up close against the window where she could lift the blind a crack, surreptitiously, longing for the sight of familiar places and, most of all, Curzon Street itself. And her young spirits rose despite themselves—once they met, face to face, surely, oh *surely* Sir Michael would listen to her? Since he had taken the trouble to offer her ransom he could not hate her entirely?

She began as best she could to pat her hair into some

159

semblance of order, having discarded the loathsome rag. Her appearance would certainly do nothing to plead her cause, she thought sadly, feeling the harsh calico against her breast and arms in the restricted space. Then another quick glance through the window set her spirit soaring—they were turning into Berkeley Square! She would look no more since a scant two minutes should bring them to his door. She strove to collect her thoughts, made well-nigh impossible as her pulses raced.

Because of the effort, she scarce noticed that they took an unconscionable time before turning into Curzon Street.

Then, sharply, the carriage drew up and for a moment her heart failed her. The two escorts bundled out and she followed, head up, smile radiant, for she was safe.

Then it struck her that both street and entry were strange, but thinking only that Sir Michael had wisely made a secret rendezvous so the villains might not know his real abode, she followed a man in the doorway who ushered her along a paved court, filled with shrubs in pots, and opened a front door at the end. With surprising agility this man pushed her inside and slammed the door, hard, in the faces of her escort who had come to receive the payment.

The servant melted away and Camilla went forward, along a thickly carpeted hall with rare paintings on the walls to an open door through which soft lamplight came and the light of a crackling fire.

Drawing a deep breath she went in, her hands held out beseechingly in front of her.

Then she froze in the doorway, her radiance become a mask of fear.

Straddling in front of the fireplace across the beautiful room stood not Sir Michael—but Caspar Randal.

Chapter Eleven

"You!" exclaimed Camilla, her very lips blanched with fear.

Sir Caspar neither moved nor spoke, merely looked over her sad disarray with evident satisfaction.

"Why did you, of all people, pay for my freedom?" asked Camilla even more unnerved by the silence and his staring. At that he laughed:

"Pay?" he laughed. "Not one penny piece would I give for your 'freedom,' my dear. Villains are fools and easily outwitted."

"I—I don't understand you, sir." Then an unlikely explanation came to her and, from her own love of truth and fair dealing she went on: "Or did you—perhaps wish to atone for the grievous wrong you did me at the Ball?" She managed a tremulous little smile.

"Ha! A 'grievous wrong,' you call it?" he sneered. *"I am the one who has been wronged and cheated by your haughty ways—and you a mere chit of a harlot!"*

Color flooded her face and her anger seethed. "I declare I am no such thing! Had you not been too—too drunken to remember, I fought off your unpleasant advances at The Crown! Indeed, you were repellent to me—and will always be."

"Stap me, the little alley cat has claws," he drawled with a smile. "It whets my appetite, I declare."

Camilla took a step back but he moved to her side like lightning, pushing his face close to hers, his eyes blazing.

"I meant to have you then and I have not changed, *Countess*—for at last you are in my power, my prisoner. Not a living soul in *your* world knows that you are here! And expect no help from those thieves—they'll have taken to their heels and run for their lives!"

Camilla stiffened every muscle in her body, resolved to resist him to the death if need be. Hatred flamed in her wide gray eyes. "I shall never give in, never I swear!"

"You have no choice," he said hotly. "You set some kind of spell upon me, Camilla, then fanned it by spurning me publicly these many weeks. In favor of *Monford,* of all people! He has earned my hatred, too, and he shall not have what I want for after this night is done he will not touch you."

His breath smelt of wine even at this early hour, and he did not move back but there was still room between them for Camilla to press her arms across her breast. Unfortunately she brushed his sleeve and, in fury, he forced her arms down and this time pressed his narrow lips painfully on to hers. Camilla gritted her teeth offering all the resistance in her power as she tried to raise her hands to beat him off. But his combined loathing and longing gave him the strength of ten men and, had his mouth not still been on hers, trying to force a response, she must have cried out at the renewed pain in her already sadly bruised arms.

She stumbled back a little, but there was no escape as his arms caught her and pulled her savagely against him.

Frantically she tried to clearly remember the hall: it was certainly wide and not very long—somewhere the manservant who had admitted her must be behind a door; surely, surely he would help her? Then she remembered his look as he slammed the front door in the face of her escort and knew he would do nothing. But the front door itself? Had he latched it behind her? No, surely he had been in too great a hurry . . . if only she could reach it in some way . . . .

Maddened by her stiffness in his embrace, Sir Caspar reached a hand up between them and caught the rough neck of her dress, ripping it so sharply in his frenzy that the harsh material gave and tore, half revealing her breast.

And still she struggled, edging, edging back and dragging him with her, which he did not notice in his determination to force her surrender. By then her mouth was bruised and swollen with the pressure and he was making headway—she could taste his breath in her mouth and felt a surge of nausea.

Summoning all her remaining strength, which was fast ebbing, she beat her fists against his back and he raised his face to laugh at her. "The more you struggle the sweeter my victory!" he muttered thickly.

But, in that blessed moment when she drew a deep breath, she saw from the pictures she had noticed on her way in that they must be scarce two paces, now, from the door. She dared not think how she might wrench it open with both arms imprisoned, nor that the latch might have sprung to of itself—to her it was salvation and reach it she would, indeed *must*.

Sir Caspar's baseness came to her aid for, realizing that her long white throat was fully exposed and the soft flesh above her breast, he raised a hand to tear the dress still further and she got her right hand behind her. His mouth moved down to the base of her throat and so, unheeding, he stumbled another two paces back without noticing anything amiss.

With a lift of her heart, Camilla felt the door almost on them. Throwing her head back in apparent submission she prayed for her purpose that he would not look up as she dragged him the final step back. Then her hand furtively reached for the handle . . . and found it.

The door was thick but through it she could swear she heard the sound of muffled footsteps—or was it the

163

drumming in her ears? With the last of her strength she turned the handle, but with Caspar's weight on her she was powerless to pull it inward. She screamed—to her a faint, forlorn sound, yet it must have carried far enough.

Suddenly, the door was being pressed, hard, from outside and so forceful was the pressure and so bemused by wine and passion Sir Caspar that, before he realized what was happening, the weight of the door had knocked the two of them backward as it swung open.

As she swooned, Camilla saw the beloved face of Sir Michael, dark with anger, and she murmured his name . . . .

She knew no more until she found herself outside, cradled in the loving arms of Hannah Fernaby, her soft, familiar voice crooning soothing words above her head: "There, there, my little one—ye're safe now, praise be, safe wi' me and that noble lord as loves ye true . . . come, I'll take ye out to his carriage."

She made to support Camilla since to carry her was beyond Mrs. Fernaby's strength at that moment, so great had been her fear. But suddenly Camilla came to her full senses: "Oh, Mama! You—and Sir Michael! I never thought to see him again—is he not angered with me?"

"Angered? Why, he's neither slept nor ate since you vanished last night! If ever a man loved with all his being I swear 'tis he!"

Camilla let her head sink again for a moment against the kindly shoulder for the floor still had a regrettable tendency to rise and fall before her weary eyes. Then: "Thank God, oh, how *much* I have to be thankful for," she said fervently. "But I will not stir from this spot until we know what has befallen Sir Michael." She shivered at recent hateful memories. "The man inside—Sir Caspar Randal, no less, who frequents The Crown—is a veritable savage, a beast . . . oh, Mama, I was in poor case before but now . . . what will my dear love think of me?"

"He cares nothing fer looks, child," Mrs. Fernaby assured her. "Dear Lord, we might've found ye drowned in t'river or worse in those evil by-ways. Oh, Camilla, I dare not think o' it," and a sob broke in her voice. It was Camilla's turn to comfort as best she could in her weakened state. But surprisingly her arms were less painful as they enclosed the kindly soul she loved so dearly.

"You must not weep for me, Mama dearest—'tis all over now. At least . . ." she cast a fearful eye at the door Sir Michael had closed firmly behind him, and she whispered: "What may be taking place in there? I'm mighty frightened for him—I vow Sir Caspar was possessed of the devil himself this night!"

She took an uncertain step forward as though to reenter that dreaded place, but Hannah caught her back:

"No, no, child—Sir Michael ordered me to take you right out to his carriage, away from all possible danger. This is a matter betwixt men and ye *must not* intervene."

Camilla came to her senses once more. To go in would be sheer folly and might ruin Sir Michael's plan. Yet to wait was nigh unbearable.

Clinging together, the two women prayed silently as they had never prayed before that he might be safe. For Camilla, at least, knew that Caspar Randal was not above stealthy murder or any other foul means to gain his own ends. This alerted her to the danger if he proved to be the one to come through the door.

"Mama—I entreat you that *you* go to the carriage. I declare you shall not run into danger through my fault and there you will be safe. I *pray* you."

Mrs. Fernaby drew herself up proudly. "What? Ye'd have me run off when danger threatens? Fie on ye, Camilla, I know yer noble man will be victor whatever they be up to. And if worst comes to worst then two of us will be a sight stronger than one—especially with you half swooning even now!"

Camilla smiled wanly. "Mama, you are a veritable angel! Pray do not think it to be a weakness," she added urgently, "for 'tis but . . . but . . ."

"Aye." Hannah's voice was grim. "Ye've been in the

hands o' cut-throats and worse—now this! 'Tis a miracle ye've still the strength to stand upright."

They waited and listened, but no sound came from the chambers. Knowing the strength of her would-be assailant, Camilla knew fear as she had never experienced it for herself. For it was *Michael* behind that hated door—her one true love and her veritable life who was facing the unimaginable for her sake.

Inside Caspar Randal's chambers, Sir Michael, his sword drawn, looked with loathing at the disarray of clothing and slackened mouth displayed by Randal. Monford spoke harshly:

"I have come to kill you, Randal, for the rat you are. But 'twill not be done in cold blood. I challenged you at the Ball and I challenge you now—take up your blade."

Caspar fumbled at first, then steel entered him: he would still triumph for his skill with a rapier was considerable. Once he was armed, Sir Michael formally saluted the enemy with his own blade, then lunged with all his strength. It caught Caspar across the right arm, ripping his elegant sleeve and drawing blood. He retreated into the drawing room—still most seductively lit—but it also banished the last traces of his earlier lust: the man he had hated for so long should be the victim and *he* would still carry off the prize!

To and fro they thrust and parried over the rich carpet, ornaments sent flying, and a quick riposte by Randal slashed his rival's coat—surely the blow had reached the heart? But in the next moment Monford had his point at Caspar's throat and slowly, inevitably, forced him down on his knees. Then he spoke, his voice taut:

"Why, Randal? I demand to know why you have behaved as a blackguard? God knows I have never harmed you and as to my lady Camilla de Courville, she scarce knows you!"

Through clenched teeth the reply came: "Oh, but she

does indeed! I declare she *was* the doxy at The Crown—I have Fernaby's witness to prove it—and she repudiated me, scarred my honor as a gentleman! 'Tis past forgiving."

"Your honor?" Sir Michael's voice seared like ice. "What Honor persecutes a lady who refuses his unwelcome advances? You forget that I, too, was present, and witnessed that unseemly encounter! Get up!"

Unsteadily, Randal rose and, his voice high-pitched, screamed: "At least grant that I recovered Camilla from those thieves! Instead of my valet I hired a prize wrestler to receive them when their hands were held out for money. He reeled them back from my door, one atop the other." His chuckle was hoarse for he was afraid and his throat somewhat constricted. "So now she has become a free booty between the two of us!"

The very word "booty" inflamed Sir Michael to near madness—for his Camilla, his dear love, to be so described added a power to his sword never achieved before.

Randal stood facing him, defiantly straddling the fire as he had done when Camilla ran to greet him in mistake.

With a final lunge, carrying all his strength, Sir Michael aimed his point at Randal's heart and found its mark fair and square. The figure crumpled down before him, an expression of surprise still in the eyes.

Caspar Randal was dead.

When Camilla's courage and hope had reached their lowest ebb, the door opened and she started forward.

Sir Michael came out slowly, still sheathing his sword. His handsome face was ashen and there was an ugly slash down the left side of his dark green coat.

"Sir Caspar Randal will not bother you again," he announced flatly.

"You have been hurt," cried Camilla, rushing to his side, all her ills and weaknesses quite forgotten in her relief at seeing Sir Michael still alive. "Oh, my love, how badly are you wounded?"

Sir Michael looked down at his coat in some surprise. "Not at all, I think—an attempt but no more. He kept his rapier to hand so, in that way, 'twas a fair fight—but not a duel of honor." Then he looked at Camilla's white, bruised face in some alarm and he raised a hand to caress her cheek very gently. "My poor little love—what you have suffered bears no thinking."

"Now—now that you are safe I have clean forgot it all," she declared, and knew it to be true. "We will go at once to your house so that your Mama, Augusta, and I may care for you—for I swear you *have* been hurt."

He smiled wryly. "Alas, no gentle caring for me, my dear love. I have killed a man. Do you not understand? I am honor bound to give myself into the hands of the law."

"Oh, *no*," Camilla gasped, horrified, "if ever man killed in the name of honor it was you this night, Michael. I will *not* have you suffer further through my own foolishness! Why had I but had more faith in your love—and that of others—this wretched business need never have taken place. Oh, Michael I implore you, do not take that course until we have talked long and seriously."

"Aye, come ye both out to the carriage," said Mrs. Fernaby with a rare note of authority in her voice. "Ye're both run widdershins, I swear, 'neath all the emotion and suffering of this time. Come."

With his arm 'round her shoulders, Sir Michael and Camilla followed her, meek as children, although Sir Michael knew that he was only postponing his duty as a gentleman. Men of his class and standing were never hunted as murderers—the law trusted them to surrender themselves and make a voluntary confession.

The faithful driver of Sir Michael's carriage had dismounted from his high seat and hastened to help the three woebegone people inside to comfort. For he had never seen his master so pale, and the women—well!

"Is it home, sir?" he asked solicitously.

But he was answered, to his surprise, by the young Countess:

"Not for a few minutes," she said clearly. "Forgive us but there are urgent matters to discuss."

For a plan was forming in her mind—a plan so simple and yet very daring for it risked all on one throw.

However, she had forgotten Sir Michael's absolute masculinity, his care, and protectiveness. As she opened her mouth to speak he forestalled her, turning to face her fully in the dimness of the carriage.

"My beloved, that you must be bruised and sore, I know, but tell me truthfully—has anyone deeply harmed you? I must know, for I have gone through such torment of mind since you ran from the Ball."

She could see his dark eyes, warm in the reflection from the carriage lamps at each side, and her heart dissolved with love. "No, my darling, I swear it. And oh, Michael, can you ever forgive my stupidity? 'Twas all my own fault, everything that passed, for I was selfish and felt such shame after Sir Caspar's words. I—I could not believe that you could still love me. I declare, all the while I was held captive, I felt that it was a just punishment."

"Camilla!" His voice deepened in reproach and he gently drew her against his shoulder; he ached to kiss her, but would not inflict even the lightest touch on her face for the present. "What kind of love would it be that faltered at every lie? 'Twould be utterly unworthy of you, I vow. No, my deep regret is that I was so anxious for news of you that I was not able to renew my challenge to that—that dastardly creature, and call him out as I had sworn to do at dawn this very morning."

"That makes your sword fight just now a true and noble act. Pray, pray see, my dearest, that 'twas but a duel indoors instead of on some field. You *cannot* accuse yourself of murder!"

He sighed, "Even you cannot sway me from my duty, little love. It is cruel indeed that, having found you at last, we must so soon be parted again. For it *was* murder, committed in the heat of hatred and I cannot be sorry that the snake is dead. But, on my honor as a gentleman, I must go to the Law."

Mrs. Fernaby had sat mouse-still in the far corner as they talked, her heart heavy with grief for the fine young couple. Now she said softly: " 'Tis for the best, Camilla, and the Law will be merciful when they know the truth."

"No," Camilla spoke very firmly. "At least hear my plan, Michael. It is unusual but will at once absolve your honor from any stain and quite certainly save your life!"

He raised a surprised, inquiring eyebrow, so Camilla hurried on: "Let us drive immediately to Carlton House and seek audience with His Royal Highness! He *is* the supreme Law of England and, if Mrs. Fitzherbert speaks true, he has a warm, sympathetic heart. Do not think I am run mad, my darling"—she clutched his hands to press her point—"He—he showed me much favor at my presentation and I warrant Mrs. Fitzherbert will be on our side."

"Our side?"

"But of course," she cried. "Can you not see that every dreadful thing that has happened is my fault? I mean to remain staunch at your side whatever action you take. If killing that—*that brute* has besmirched your honor, you only did it to save mine!"

She paused, holding her breath, for she knew she must press no further. Sir Michael was very much his own man but, as he stared away from her at the darkened pavement beyond the window, she did not release his hands. Silently she prayed fervently that he might agree to her suggestion. Mrs. Fernaby held her breath, too. It was as if their whole future hung in the balance, resting on Sir Michael's decision. At last he said, doubtfully:

"Prinny will be in a mighty temper if he is disturbed," he said. Camilla let her breath go in a great sigh of thankfulness. She had won! "Besides," Sir Michael continued, "he may be giving a dinner for his own circle—we cannot appear as we look at this moment!"

170

Camilla tossed her small head. "I declare I intend to appear just as I am! This—this disgraceful gown was torn by Caspar Randal, the bruise on my mouth is further proof. What weight will my words carry if I am tastefully gowned, coiffed, and my injuries skillfully covered? 'Tis useless to ask me to change my mind."

Sir Michael smiled. "I see I have found a girl not only of great beauty and charm but of great spirit as well." Then he called up to his driver, "To Carlton House!"

The drive lasted scarce five minutes and, during that time, no one spoke. Camilla knew a sudden pang of fear —what if the prince proved to be angered after all? Could it be that she was running her love into yet more danger? She tried to remember the large, benign figure who had complimented her so delightfully at the Ball. Then her heart took comfort—since there was evidently no state occasion that night, surely Mrs. Fitzherbert would be present and perchance she, too, still bore affection for Camilla . . . a woman with her great heart must hear the lovers' plea with kindliness . . .

The carriage drew up. Mrs. Fernaby shrank still further into her corner as Sir Michael got out and helped Camilla down. The great doors were closed, with a sentry on duty. Ignoring him, Sir Michael led Camilla up the steps and pulled the golden bell cord.

"I have allowed you your way," Sir Michael smiled down at the dear girl on his arm. "Now I crave that you let me plead my own cause *if* we are granted audience."

She had no time to answer since two footmen, bewigged and powdered, opened the door.

"Pray tell His Royal Highness that Sir Michael Monford and the Countess de Courville beg a brief private audience —and convey my apologies for disturbing him at this hour." One footman bowed and departed with the message. The other stood watch over the, to him, disreputable couple. It would give him pleasure to throw them out if the prince returned an abrupt refusal as he most surely would.

The first man seemed to be gone an unconscionably long time and Camilla felt her nervousness returning. Then, at last, he returned and with another bow and, this time, a faint smile, he said:

"Please to follow me."

Normally, Camilla would have looked about her with deep interest for they were being escorted to the prince's private rooms and the passages seemed even more ornate than the main hall that led to the ballroom, but her mind was too anxious, too full at the moment.

Stopping at a gold and white door, the footman asked: "Whom should I announce, sir?"

"Sir Michael Monford and the Countess de Courville," said Camilla clearly before Sir Michael could speak. The door was flung open and they were announced in ringing tones.

They advanced, hand in hand. The prince and Mrs. Fitzherbert were quite alone, playing patience at an inlaid table. His Highness was pouting, furious at having his one quiet evening so rudely disturbed. But Mrs. Fitzherbert stared, at first with disbelief for, indeed, Camilla could scarce be recognized in such poor garb—and that torn— her hair in disarray and her face heavily bruised. But suddenly her eyes lighted and she sprang up, tilting the table to the prince's further annoyance since the difficult patience had been going in his favor and he loved to win.

"Camilla! Oh, my poor, poor child what has befallen?" she cried, opening her motherly arms in glad welcome. Gratefully, Camilla ran into them and allowed herself to be most warmly embraced. "Oh, how I have waited and watched this morning with my dear friend the Marquise," continued the grand lady. "I declare, she is quite distracted. Have you seen her, I trust?"

"Alas, not yet," admitted Camilla. "For the business that brings us here so inopportunely, I fear, is most urgent." She broke away from the comforting arms and made a deep curtsey to the prince who was growing intrigued enough to reach his quizzing glass out of an embroidered pocket in his waistcoat. Who was this ragged chit, so eagerly received by his love? He studied Camilla for a minute, then shook his head in continued puzzlement.

Sir Michael stepped forward and bowed low. "Your royal Highness is kindness itself in granting us this brief interview—for, on my oath, we will not detain you long."

"Then, stap me, get on with it, Monford. Ye look pretty tatterdemalion yerself!"

"I have but just killed Sir Caspar Randal," said Sir Michael tonelessly. "It took place in his private chambers and, tho' he had a rapier to hand, I went in with murder in my heart."

"Eh?" the prince was obviously annoyed. "Then surely your duty lies with an officer of the law, sirrah, not with us."

Camilla could keep silent no longer. Drawing herself up she spoke, her low voice without a tremor since she was pleading for Sir Michael's life:

"Your Royal Highness will not remember me, seeing me in this sorry plight, but I am the Countess de Courville to whom you were most gracious at the Ball. During that magnificent occasion Sir Michael and I became betrothed before going in to supper. There, in a loud voice, Sir Caspar hurled insults at me and, to my eternal shame, I took fright and ran away, fearful of what might follow. Oh, my Royal Liege, I pray your forgiveness, for the ills that have befallen my dearest Sir Michael are all my fault—caused by blind foolishness."

She felt, imperceptibly, that she was receiving a glimmer of interest at last. While raising his quizzing glass again in one hand, he pinched his pouting lips with the other as though considering:

"Carry on with your tale, Countess—did you, then, run to Sir Caspar?"

"Oh, *no!*" In her horror at such a suggestion Camilla had quite forgot the formal Royal address that was supposed to preface every speech: "My one thought was to run to my foster-mother in Cheapside believing that from thenceforth all society would spurn me."

"Surely you did not misjudge Sir Michael thus?" interrupted Mrs. Fitzherbert gently.

"To my eternal shame I fear that I did," confessed Camilla and, at the same moment, gave such a glance of glowing love in his direction that the prince listened more intently. However:

"Gad, how women do gabble on," he chided a trifle testily. "I am waiting for your story, madam, all of it!"

"Yes, your Highness. I ran from this royal house like a mad thing, taking no cloak or dark covering and so—I was captured by thieves and held for ransom."

The prince opened his small eyes wide in astonishment: "In London, our capital, such goings on?"

"Indeed yes, Sire." Camilla was amazed at this glimpse of how far he was removed from his subjects but, anxious not to irritate him again, she hurried on. "The ransom was offered and a plan for my deliverance made ... I thought, hearing the money was offered by a gentleman, that it must be Sir Michael; in truth he *had* offered at once, but this other person offered twice the sum demanded."

"And also arranged an earlier assignation with the kidnappers," interrupted Sir Michael, angrily. "I swear, if I could but lay my hands on them!"

The royal eyes twinkled. "Then you would be here, no doubt, confessing ye'd done further murder!"

"Oh, your Highness, his killing of Sir Caspar was *not* murder—'twas a noble act to save my honor!" cried Camilla. "To my horror, you see, I was delivered to Sir Caspar's rooms—he did not even pay the two men escorting me, tho' they were not my captors. Then ..." her face paled and she found it hard to go on. Mrs. Fitzherbert, murmuring gentle words of affection, went to her side:

"You must tell His Royal Highness the whole of it, my dear—else how can he judge Sir Michael's deed?"

Camilla gave her a brief, wan smile of thanks and she

could see her love's hands clasped tightly in fury as she proceeded:

"He—Sir Caspar—reviled me again most cruelly and then . . . then he came right up to me and"—her voice was very quiet and she lowered her gray eyes in shame and renewed shock at the memory—"and he tried to ravage me. Indeed, I think he had run mad in that moment." She looked up again, her beautiful gray eyes so clear but troubled. "He—he tore this poor dress I was forced to wear, and I kept edging back toward the front door, bearing him with me since he did not notice. I cannot say why I felt it to be my only hope . . . but, thank the dear Lord, it was. Sir Michael had just arrived and, as I managed to turn the knob, he pushed it in with all his might, sending us both headlong to the floor. But—he had seen enough and—and I fear I swooned." She could say no more.

"Oh, my poor, poor child." Mrs. Fitzherbert put an arm around the slim, trembling shoulders as Sir Michael stepped forward and spoke:

"I confess, Sire, that I have never been so blinded by rage; I would have run him through, there and then as he lay, but he sprang up and seized a rapier—and I was glad that he, too, was armed yet he was still dazed by his vile passions so his aim was far from true. I killed him cleanly." He bowed his proud head. "I cannot deny my guilt, nor excuse it except . . ."

"Except that, but for you my dearest, my entire life would be besmirched and, I swear, I must have killed myself for shame." Camilla turned to the Prince.

"Highness, now both our lives are in your hands for you know the whole truth"—she met his eyes fearlessly, although her heart was pounding against her ribs—"I beseech your grace and mercy, for only you can extend the royal pardon to Sir Michael. He is most noble in every thought, word and deed."

Mrs. Fitzherbert's arm tightened around her for support —she could feel the rapid heartbeats being so close to the frightened girl. Her own eyes met those of her royal husband, briefly, and in them was her own pleading for this cause.

The silence seemed to last a lifetime as the young lovers waited, their lives in the balance. The prince was known for his capricious moods that could change as swiftly as the flicker of lightning. And his face gave away none of his thoughts as he looked, piercingly, from one to the other.

In truth, the silence lasted scarce a full minute before, with a rare warmth in his smile, he gave the verdict:

"Cold-blooded killing is a crime, as well you know, Monford, but this was no such thing! I have never cared for Randal myself and what I have heard tonight confirms my own judgement. For such behavior to a lady he deserved to die like a rat. You have my full pardon, Monford—and I wish you and the countess a long and happy life in marriage."

Sir Michael bowed low in gratitude, but Camilla went further in her heartfelt thankfulness. She ran forward, curtseyed low and kissed the plump hand that lay, beringed, on the arm of the chair.

The prince looked down in gratified surprise. "My dear young Countess!" Then he chuckled, "Get yerself home and pay yer respects in more suitable guise on the morrow."

The prince watched the two bedraggled, yet radiant, lovers leave his presence, then he issued swift orders. He instructed that Principal Officers of the Law were to attend him immediately, for he was deeply shocked by what had taken place in his own city of London.

Within twenty-four hours, despite her boast to Camilla that the Law would never trace her, Sal Perkins and her confederates were caught and cast into Newgate Prison, there to await judgement and just punishment for their crime of kidnapping and extorting money. Sal's "friends" were only too anxious to give her away if it meant saving their skins and, above all, shifting the Law from their own shady territory.

Chapter Twelve

The reunion at the de Fouchets' mansion was highly emotional. The Marquise, after a gasp of disbelief followed by joy hastened to embrace Camilla most fondly, murmuring her name over and over again. She was followed by the Marquis, tears streaming unchecked down his old face. As he saluted Camilla on both cheeks he cried:

"My child! my dear, dear little Claudette-Camilla!" Then he blew his nose, adding between laughter and tears: "How fortunate to be French at such a moment—the English despise the release of tears!"

Both old people embraced Sir Michael, then warmly shook Mrs. Fernaby by the hand, well aware of how much was owed to her in rescuing Camilla, whatever her danger had been.

Then the little French clock musically chimed the hour of eight and Mrs. Fernaby stared at it, horrified:

"Forgive me—I declare I must go—must hurry! My husband will have taken no tea and now the tavern will be open. Oh! He will be in such a taking and angry . . . ." Her face had paled and a tremor shook her as she alone knew the terrors that awaited her.

Camilla, knowing her fear, swiftly caught her hands: "No, no Mama, you must not return there after all that we owe you! We shall protect you—care for you . . ."

The Marquise interrupted in silvery tones:

"I agree, Camilla. Mrs. Fernaby, we know you little and yet through Camilla, we know you well and understand how much you suffer so bravely. I have long sought an English housekeeper who might bear with la mode Française and not grow impatient. I declare it will give us much pleasure if you would stay here?"

Camilla flushed with gratitude and delight, turning back eagerly to her dear mother. "Mama, did you hear? Oh, is it not the perfect ending to this terrible day that has turned to such delight?"

But Mrs. Fernaby was twisting her thin hands together in some agitation. "My Lady, ye're kindness touches me deep, but I would not bring trouble to your beautiful house and I—I fear my husband will find me and make trouble. Then—there are my things, they are poor but I would not lose them."

It was Sir Michael who clinched the matter. Resting a hand on her shoulder he said gently, "Mother Fernaby —for to me you will always be that from now on, pray set your troubles behind you. Is it not our turn to care for you?" He looked long and adoringly at Camilla as he added, "I know my future bride will agree when I declare that later, when we have our own family, we would trust no one but you to take charge of the nursery wing. If you tend the future generations of Monfords as well as you have brought up Camilla, they could ask for no better start in life."

Camilla's eyes, glowing with fervent love and gratitude, thanked him as she gently kissed the tearful cheek. "There, Mama, I declare your happiness is all planned for you. Never, never again are you to face fear and torment. Why, we are all so joyous—yet, how could that continue during this evening, knowing that you might be in very danger of your life? Besides, I shall send a servant for your things— I know just where they are to be found, so pray accept the charming offer of the Marquise, 'twill make this day quite perfect."

Mrs. Fernaby was beyond speech but, shyly, she bobbed a little curtsey to the Marquise and managed a tremulous smile. Then, turning to Camilla, she said almost briskly, "Come, child, let me tend those bruises and gown you fittingly for your betrothal evening."

Meekly, her eyes dancing, Camilla took her hand and led her out and upstairs to her bedroom.

By the week's end, Camilla's bruises and abrasions had all vanished—with each day so golden and filled with happiness, how could it be otherwise?

Not only had the Marquis de Fouchet given his glad consent to the marriage, but Lady Monford also seemed pleased.

"It's high time that Michael took a wife," she said, "and his choice could not be more fitting. Come, dear girl, and allow me to embrace you."

Augusta, naturally, was overjoyed and, turning to her brother she said, "Now, at last, perhaps you will take time to hear my tidings and to see my dear Mr. Edwards! We, too, are deep in love but my, he is so proper! Nothing will do but he must have your consent before any betrothal is formally made."

"Quite right, I declare," he replied with mock sternness, tho' his dark eyes twinkled. "I must consider the matter!"

"Don't you dare," exclaimed Augusta and Camilla laughed:

"Have no fears, do you not know how he loves to tease?"

The only argument remaining was where the marriage of Sir Michael and his beautiful countess should be celebrated. Lady Monford wished for it to be at the little church on their country estate. "The tenants will make such a day of it—I swear you cannot consider holding it elsewhere, Michael," she stated firmly.

But he wished for a far grander ceremony. He longed

for his lovely bride to be acclaimed by all members of society—to kill forever the last lingering whispers among the ill-natured that still lurked, here and there, after the unfortunate scene at the Royal Ball.

Camilla took no sides, for her the wondrous miracle of becoming Michael's wife lit her every moment, waking or sleeping.

Then, from a clear sky, the decision was made for them. Mrs. Fitzherbert arrived to call on the Marquise, her kindly face filled with suppressed excitement:

"My dear Friend, I bring news—such news! I have oft told you that my prinny has a warm heart beneath his foibles and now he is proving it. He took such a fancy to our little Camilla when she appeared in the guise of a beggar maid to plead with him that he now wishes to give her a royal wedding, no less!"

At that moment Camilla came in, slim and elegant in a crimson velvet riding habit, a small tricorn hat held with fine veiling framing her shining hair and radiant face. Sir Michael insisted on giving her riding lessons each day, for he declared:

"You would not have me tear my heart in two at having to leave your side whenever I go riding, would you my darling? Yet riding is in my very blood and I vow you will make a fine horsewoman . . . why," he laughed, "you may even come to enjoy it as I do once you overcome your fear of horses!"

She had blushed, then, remembering her shame as he introduced her to his magnificent stallion and, when it reared and whinnied, she had flinched back, unable to help herself.

Now, to her surprise and joy, she was coming to love the gentle, chestnut mare that he had given her and she no longer backed away from Spartacus.

She curtsied and then ran to embrace Mrs. Fitzherbert who returned the affection then held her away to study her.

"What a royal bride ye'll make," she declared, smiling.

180

"A *what?*" Camilla was bewildered.

Mrs. Fitzherbert went on smoothly, pleased at this reaction to her surprise. "The Prince Regent wishes you to be married from Windsor Castle in the Royal Chapel. Furthermore, since you have no father, he insists on giving you away himself." She turned to the Marquis who had sat silent in his big armchair. "That is, if you, Marquis, as her guardian, have no objection?" That this was pure courtesy they all realized, for the prince, having made up his mind on any issue, would not brook any objections.

The old Marquis smiled. "I shall be honored, and relieved, pray reassure His Royal Highness. 'Twould be a sorry start for Camilla to be led up the aisle on the arm of a hobbling rheumatic such as myself!"

Camilla still found the whole thing beyond belief.

"You mean—His Highness was not offended after all at our intrusion on your privacy that evening?"

"At first, of course he was," replied Mrs. Fitzherbert firmly. "Then your tale so intrigued him that he has referred to it constantly." She hesitated. "Do the common people really behave so?"

Camilla felt embarrassed, the question was as direct as it was unexpected. "I believe—" she began slowly, then gathered strength—"there is such dire poverty in the East End of London, that they cannot help but contrast the riches of court circles with their own straits. If thieving is all they can do then many regard it as their right. Oh" —she looked distressed—"you will not repeat that to His Royal Highness, I pray—for I would not have them persecuted. I—I spent my childhood in their midst and, tho' I abhorred such actions of course, I could not easily condemn it."

The elderly favorite, morgannatically married to the royal person, was serious. "No, child—you underrate the tact that has made me his trusted confidante. But, if a chance occurs, I swear, for your sake, I will try to influence him to a more liberal attitude to his subjects."

181

"Oh, Mrs. Fitzherbert, if you only can! They could be so easily swayed, I know."

"Now," said that august lady, "let's talk of happier things . . . your wedding."

Even Lady Monford was placated by this surprising turn of events: to see her only son and heir married in the Royal Chapel stretched beyond her wildest dreams. They would hold a later celebration on the estate when all their people should come and be feasted.

In the de Fouchet household chaos might have reigned but for the calming influence of Mrs. Fernaby, now suitably attired in black silk with a frilly muslin apron and a silver chain girdle from which hung the keys to the many still-rooms, dairy and pantries. Her rule over the household was firm but kindly and her fame as a heroine had preceded her, so that even the stately butler received her as an equal.

To Camilla, fraught amid a welter of fittings for her wedding gown and all her trousseau, the presence of her mama was soothing. She even dared to calm Monsieur Paul and the Marquise when they were being at their most French and temperamental.

Meantime, Sir Michael wrote a letter of loyalty and gratitude to the prince for his truly regal gesture. Such a magnificent wedding would put paid forever to the few remaining spiteful whispers about Camilla. Indeed, Michael smiled a trifle grimly to himself, as he thought of the way every member of the *ton* would be angling for an invitation to the great occasion.

And, despite the protests of the Marquise, Camilla set aside one whole day to be with her betrothed. Passionately she wished for a long, quiet talk together during which she could relate all her past life with its vicissitudes and lowliness, so that nothing that befell in the future could ever dismay or shock him.

He was delighted at her suggestion that they spend a day together, far from all the wedding preparations, and they drove down to Richmond in his carriage to a charming spot by the river. There they could stroll or just sit and talk without disturbance and there was an old hostelry nearby where he was wont to go for a simple meal after riding for hours in Richmond Park.

Camilla found herself unexpectedly shy at first, it was such bliss to be alone with Michael at last and her story seemed to her sordid, to say the least. But he was eager to hear it for every aspect of his love's life but further enhanced her courage in his estimation.

When, however, she came to her time at Maison Castle it was his turn to make a shameful confession:

"My dearest heart—to think I saw you, more, I even felt I recognized you, yet I was still too blind and proud to admit the truth! Camilla"—he turned to her and clasped her slender hands—"in your tale I find not only nothing to forgive but all that is worthy of my deepest homage. But, for myself, there are no excuses. I dare not even crave your understanding."

Tenderly she stretched up and kissed his lean, solemn cheek: "You do not need to ask, my darling, since you have it in full measure. We live in an age bound by convention—by what our position at birth dictates. I would not have you a traitor to your kind, my darling, for you are the noblest, most honorable man I have ever known."

After that they succumbed to the longing for lovers' talk, for tender embraces and dreams of the future. At last he declared:

"Now there are no more secret places between us, my love—our hearts are one single open book."

"No secrets," she echoed softly as he took her in his arms, but, over his shoulder her eyes twinkled: for there was one that should go with her to the grave: the vigils on the corner of Curzon Street when she, a poor shop girl, had first lost her heart to this man who loved her so wondrously. It was the first sign of her maturing femininity and her heart rejoiced.

He led her to the hostelry where they laughed and teased each other over the excellent but simple fare, grown quite light-headed with happiness.

Since the prince had insisted on the wedding taking place before he left for his summer sojourn at Brighton, time grew ever shorter but sempstresses, milliners, and shoemakers worked with such a will that at last all was ready.

"Camilla," chided the Marquise, "I know you are deep in love, *Cherie,* but I fancy you do not show Monsieur Paul the gratitude that is his due. I think a petite gesture is called for!"

Instantly Camilla was all contrition: "Oh, Marquise, I have thanked him indeed—but, perchance, a visit to his salon with a handsome gift and posies for the girls who have worked such wonders might be fitting?"

The Marquise clapped her small hands and smiled. "The very thing, I declare! Now . . . *mais oui,* a case of finest champagne will do very well and you shall order the posies yourself!"

Camilla's visit turned into an almost royal progress as she was escorted through his workrooms by Monsieur Paul, beaming his delight. For the wedding gown and the trousseau were his chef d'oeuvre, the masterpiece of his career:

"And no great lady is more beautiful and élégante to show them to advantage, Countess!" It was his highest tribute.

Augusta was equally pleased with her bridesmaid's gown and, knowing that her own wedding was but a scant month ahead, with Michael to give her away and Camilla acting as Matron of Honor, the beauty that Camilla had forecast for her long weeks ago had come into full bloom. She looked radiant.

184

At last it was time for the mammoth duty of packing everything to adjourn to Windsor Castle, for all were bidden to attend a royal banquet there on the wedding eve and to remain for the night.

Over this task Mrs. Fernaby came into her own once again. Seemingly quite composed she supervised the small army of women packing the great trunks and the valises that were to accompany the bride on her honeymoon and thence to her new home, but inwardly her heart was aflutter, for she, too, was to travel to Windsor and be entrusted with dressing her beloved daughter on the great day.

Late in the evening before they were to leave, she went to Camilla's room where they could be alone. There, Camilla ran into her arms as she had done throughout her life:

"Mama dearest, I owe all this happiness to you," said the girl tenderly, a hint of tearful emotion in her voice.

"Aye, little did we think, sitting in our kitchen in what seems another life, that you would reach the very heights! Why, I swear that Sir Michael is the greatest gentleman on earth—and to be married in the Chapel Royal, with the prince at your side ... oh, 'tis a miracle beyond all our dreams!"

She, too, was growing emotional and Camilla drew her down beside her on the velvet settee. There they talked quietly, for the last time, of the past with sweet tears as well as laughter, until Camilla said:

"Yet the crowning of it all, for me, is that you are happy at last—and free, Mama! Fernaby has not approached you?"

"He attempted it once," replied Mrs. Fernaby grimly, then smiled. "I vow he will never try it again! No, he is sunk in the trough of his own making, I hear—drinking hard and finding the women of the streets more lively company than I!"

"He deserves no better," said Camilla warmly.

Then Mrs. Fernaby remembered her duties and stood

185

up. "Now, my child, 'tis time you were in bed! I need not wish you glad dreams, for they will be naught else—and ye must be glorious as the dawn itself on the morrow."

Meekly, Camilla obeyed. Not for her the oft-feared sleeplessness and nerves of a bride. Her heart winged so eagerly to her bridegroom that she only longed for the hours to pass until he was her true husband.

The royal banquet at Windsor Castle was all goodwill and merriment. The prince had chosen only his own favorites to attend so, even with the de Fouchets, the Monfords, and the bride and groom, it was an intimate affair tho' none the less splendid for that. He had ordered all his own preferences—fine wines, of course, then Sturgeon's Roe—a rare new import named Caviare—a soup of Quails followed by rare Baron of beef and swans roasted on the spit and farced with herbs and spices; brandied soufflé accompanied by sweetmeats of marchpane (for he had a sweet tooth) and, finally, desserts from the royal hothouses—peaches the size of a man's palm, dark grapes, green figs and small, new-blushed apricots.

Musicians in the gallery played softly—galliardes, valses, and even the now old-fashioned minuets in tribute to the Marquis and Marquise.

Camilla appeared shy, and most becoming as a bride: her gown of finely pleated lawn over a sheath of green silk embroidered with jewelled stars and flowers claimed hushed admiration from the assembly. As she took her place between the prince and Sir Michael the royal personage whispered roguishly:

"My eloquent beggarmaid transformed into an angel! Stap me, m'dear, if ye were not promised, I swear I'd bid for ye meself!"

"Highness, you are too kind." She smiled up at him and daringly teased: "I warrant few girls could resist you!"

He was in high good humor.

"May it last," prayed Mrs. Fitzherbert, sitting on his

186

other side, for, perhaps more than any of the company, she wished Camilla's great day to go well.

Camilla woke early on her wedding morning and went to the window. It was going to be a superb summer day for a quiet white mist presaging sun, and warmth lay over the meadows beyond the gardens below. Suddenly a rose landed on the windowsill, close by her hand. Looking down she saw Sir Michael smiling up at her, informally dressed in an open-necked white lawn shirt, laced doublet and fawn breeches such as he wore on his farmlands. She smiled most lovingly back and blew him a kiss, holding the dew-spangled rose against her breast. For them to speak on their wedding morn might bring bad luck, but his gesture set her heart soaring even higher.

Soon afterward her room was invaded by happy, smiling maids, shepherded in by Mrs. Fernaby to dress her for the ceremony which was to be held at eleven o'clock. The prince had eschewed the fashionably later time of early afternoon since he intended to enjoy his luncheon to the full and not be hurried over the draughts of champagne.

Monsieur Paul had, indeed, risen to new heights in creation—for the wedding gown was such stuff as dreams are made of, as immortal Will Shakespeare had said long ago. Reverently the maids unfolded it from the muslin wraps and spread the delicate folds over the bed. It was not white but palest gold to complement her beautiful hair, the bodice embroidered with small *Fleur de Lys* in pearls and small diamonds with emeralds forming the two slender leaves surrounding each. The veil was, again, a cloud of palest golden gauze giving the effect of an aura and held in place by a wreath of orange blossoms wired in to a lovely coronet—tribute to her rank as countess which she was so gladly to surrender, for the title of Lady Monford.

Until her gowning was completed, Mrs. Fernaby firmly restrained all intruders, including the Marquise and Au-

187

gusta, anxiously waiting outside. Then, with the kiss of gratitude on her cheek from her foster-daughter, she at last opened the door to reveal the vision that was Camilla.

Fortunately, and thanks entirely to the devoted Mrs. Fitzherbert, His Royal Highness was in fine fettle. Clad in regal splendor with his breast adazzle with royal decorations he waited, a trifle impatiently, for the appearance of the girl he was to lead up to the altar. But when she came, drifting light as air down the great staircase, his mouth fell open in admiration:

"Well, well—Monford is a man to be envied!" he declared, too overcome even to swear.

Behind her came Augusta in pale blue, carrying Camilla's bouquet of golden lilies and roses while the Marquise followed resplendent in cyclamen silk and diamonds, her large hat with ospreys—she was already dabbing at her eyes with a lace kerchief.

Camilla, alone, felt no nerves and, least of all any wish for tears. After a curtsey she gracefully accepted the prince's satin arm and together they walked out of the castle and along the path to the chapel, every inch crowded with admiring servants who cheered discreetly and tossed rose petals under the bride's feet as she walked. The archbishop waited in the great doors to welcome them and then lead his procession of bishops, canons and choir ahead up to the great altar. And, while Augusta was handing Camilla her flowers and giving a deft touch here and there to her gown, a splendid fanfare of silver trumpets rang out to echo joyously around the ancient rafters—a tribute normally reserved for royalty but ordered specially for this occasion by His Royal Highness.

Then, as they entered the chapel, Camilla knew nervousness at last. It was far bigger than she expected and every seat was packed with the aristocracy, all in great finery and staring openly at the bride—the woman mostly with envy, the men with unconcealed admiration. If only she could see Michael! But the long procession of clerics ahead screened her view.

Feeling her arm tremble the prince patted it with a pudgy hand—he felt gracious and avuncular, in fact mighty pleased with himself.

At last the bishops and choir parted to go to their various chairs and stalls and Michael was there, his future brother-in-law at his side. As Camilla came toward him, he turned to face her, then held out a hand to her, his dark eyes burning with love and homage to her ethereal beauty.

As she took his dear hand, all Camilla's nerves vanished and, through the fine gauze of her veil, her gray eyes shone like stars as people and chapel alike seemed to melt away.

Sir Michael and Camilla were wrapped about by their great love, alone in perfect union as they took their solemn vows.

ABOUT THE AUTHOR
Caroline Courtney

Caroline Courtney was born in India, the youngest daughter of a British Army Colonel stationed there in the troubled years after the First World War. Her first husband, a Royal Air Force pilot, was tragically killed in the closing stages of the Second World War. She later remarried and now lives with her second husband, a retired barrister, in a beautiful 17th century house in Cornwall. They have three children, two sons and a daughter, all of whom are now married, and four grandchildren.

On the rare occasions that Caroline Courtney takes time off from her writing, she enjoys gardening and listening to music, particularly opera. She is also an avid reader of romantic poetry and has an ever-growing collection of poems she has composed herself.

Caroline Courtney is destined to be one of this country's leading romantic novelists. She has written an enormous number of novels over the years—purely for pleasure—and has never before been interested in seeing them reach publication. However, at her family's insistence she has now relented, and Warner Books is proud to be issuing a selection in this uniform edition.

DANGER...
ROMANCE...ADVENTURE

YOUR WARNER LIBRARY OF
CAROLINE COURTNEY